"Let's loo

Daniel suggested.

"Right." Jill snuggled closer to him.

He slipped his arm around her, then tilted his head back to gaze at the sky. "A person doesn't often think about the size of the universe during the day," he murmured. "But at night you get a sense of the immenseness of it. It makes me feel—"

"Reverent," Jill interjected.

"Yes, reverent," Daniel agreed. "Also humble."

Jill impulsively slid her arm around his waist, hugging him. "I don't feel humble at all. Out of all infinity, the wonderful, marvelous thing is that we're sitting here together," she said. "Don't you agree?"

He kept looking to the heavens. "For being no more than two specks in the grand scale of the universe," he said slowly, "I suppose you could say it is pretty awesome that we settled here."

"Awesome, Daniel?" Jill laughed. "It was our destiny."

Dear Reader,

Thanksgiving is the one holiday in the year where the whole family gathers for that traditional turkey dinner with all the trimmings. And who can resist just one extra helping of stuffing or pumpkin pie!

Silhouette Romance novels make perfect Thanksgiving reading. They're a celebration of family and all the traditional values we hold so dear. *And* they're about the perfect love that leads to marriage and happy-ever-afters.

This month we're featuring one of our best-loved authors, Brittany Young—not to mention the ever-popular Arlene James and Marcine Smith, and the talented Pat Tracy and Patti Standard. And to round out the month we're continuing our WRITTEN IN THE STARS series with the passionate Scorpio hero in Ginna Gray's *Sting of the Scorpion*. What a lineup! And in months to come, watch for Diana Palmer, Annette Broadrick and *all* your favorites!

The authors and editors of Silhouette Romance books strive to bring you the best in romance fiction, stories that capture the laughter, the tears—the sheer joy—of falling in love. Let us know if we've succeeded. We'd love to hear from you!

Happy Reading,

Valerie Susan Hayward
Senior Editor

MARCINE SMITH

Love
Shy

Silhouette ♥ *Romance*

Published by Silhouette Books New York

America's Publisher of Contemporary Romance

For Daryl.
And in memory of my Dad, Philip. It is so true.
Good times are not forgotten.

SILHOUETTE BOOKS
300 E. 42nd St., New York, N.Y. 10017

LOVE SHY

ISBN: 0-373-08827-2

First Silhouette Books printing November 1991

Books by Marcine Smith

Silhouette Romance

Murphy's Law #589
Waltz with the Flowers #659
The Perfect Wife #683
Just Neighbors #716
The Two of Us #767
Love Shy #827

Silhouette Desire

Never a Stranger #364

MARCINE SMITH

lives on a farm in northwest Iowa with her husband and three of their four sons. She loves reading, writing romances, watching baseball, basketball and football, long drives through the Iowa/South Dakota countryside and the smell of freshly mown hay. But her favorite things are sharing the porch swing with her husband at dusk on a summer's day, watching the sun set and listening to the corn grow.

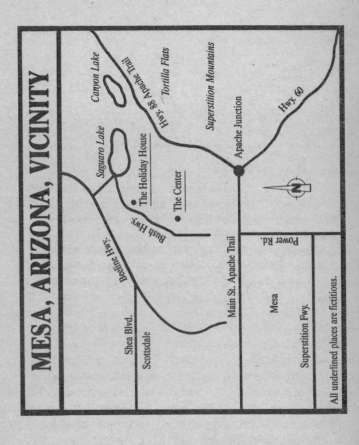

MESA, ARIZONA, VICINITY

Canyon Lake

Saguaro Lake

Tortilla Flats

Hwy. 88 Apache Trail

Superstition Mountains

The Holiday House

The Center

Apache Junction

Hwy. 60

Beeline Hwy.

Bush Hwy.

Shea Blvd.

Scottsdale

Main St. Apache Trail

Power Rd.

Mesa

Superstition Fwy.

All underlined places are fictitious.

Prologue

After three weeks as the administrator of the North Cactus Senior Citizens' Center in Mesa, Jill already dreaded the hour commute to work.

She seldom arrived back at her rented house in Phoenix before seven; often it was eight. It was even later tonight and she was bone tired by the time she turned into her driveway. Only when she saw her neighbor and landlady, Mrs. Chatham, framed in the front window of her house did she recall that earlier in the day Mrs. Chatham had called the center.

Shauna Gallagor, the social director, had taken the message because Jill had been busy at the time. It was short and sweet: Mrs. Chatham wanted to speak to Jill the *moment* she arrived home. Jill wasn't surprised that Mrs. Chatham was leaving nothing to chance.

By the time Jill had parked in the carport, Mrs. Chatham had come from her house, circled the cactus bed in her front yard, crossed Jill's yard and was standing at the front door, ramrod straight, a formidable barrier.

This did not bode well, Jill decided. She grabbed her purse and attaché case and slid from the car.

"Hello, Mrs.—"

"You've stretched my patience the positive limit, young lady," Mrs. Chatham snapped.

Right, Jill thought. It did not bode well. "Is there a problem, Mrs. Chatham?" she asked.

"You assured me when Chester moved in that he would only be here a week. It's been *two,*" Mrs. Chatham said. "I'm tired of having the house used like a motel."

Before taking the position of administrator at the senior citizens' center, Jill had been a social worker. While it was true that she'd occasionally opened her home to people who needed temporary assistance, she hadn't used the house like a motel.

"Mrs. Chatham," Jill said reasonably, "I recall only three times—"

"One woman had children who picked flowers from my flowering hedgehog," Mrs. Chatham stated. She slammed her fingers on her broad hips. "Another woman had six children and those kids built sand castles in *my* yard."

Mrs. Chatham had forgotten that Jill had spent a week raking the yard back into shape. And the poor little darlings who had picked the flowers from the hedgehog had been pricked for their efforts.

Mrs. Chatham frowned. "Then there was Mr. Moore—what happened that night you watched him for his daughter?"

"Mr. Moore suffers from senile dementia," Jill explained for the fifth or sixth time. "I should have known better than to think he would watch television while I fixed supper."

"He walked into my kitchen! *Unclothed!* He frightened me so badly I nearly had a heart attack." Mrs. Chatham dramatized by placing her hand over her heart.

If Mrs. Chatham thought Jill stretched her patience to the limit, Jill had news for her. Of all the people she had encountered over the years, Mrs. Chatham stood alone in her ability to test Jill's patience.

"Mr. Moore didn't realize he'd undressed," she stated. "He isn't responsible for his actions."

"So Mr. Moore has problems," Mrs. Chatham grudgingly admitted, adding quickly, "but what about that parrot you kept for Mrs. Grady when she flew back east to attend a funeral? That bird was disgusting!"

Jill hid her smile. Mrs. Grady was a genteel old woman. It came as a shock to discover that her bird cursed a blue streak.

"I'll admit the parrot had a bad habit, but the bird wasn't being personal when it called you names. It cursed whenever the doorbell rang."

Mrs. Chatham was not buying that simple logic. Her lips pursed. "And now we have Chester."

"Chester doesn't wander. He's obedient. And he certainly doesn't call people names."

"He's a pig."

"He's a *potbellied* pig. A very small pig. And the reason he's still here is that his owners are having trouble finding a place in Seattle," Jill said. "As soon as they do, they'll send for him."

"No," Mrs. Chatham said. She waggled a finger at Jill. "I've made up my mind. Your rent is paid until the end of the month, then Chester goes. Or you go."

"The first of November? Two weeks?"

"That's my last word," Mrs. Chatham stated, and then bustled away.

Chapter One

An hour before the center opened the next morning, Jill was at the credenza in her office preparing the first of several pots of coffee that would be consumed throughout the day.

From time to time she glanced out the window to see whether or not Shauna had arrived. Shauna had graduated from college in May. This was her first job, but she was handling it like an old pro, offering a variety of activities that provided something for everyone. It was no easy task when one considered the broad range of physical and mental abilities of the seniors who frequented the center.

Everything had been going quite nicely, thank you, Jill thought, until Mrs. Chatham decided to give her the boot. To complicate matters Sara Bolthom had called last night to say that she and her husband had found a house outside Seattle but it would be at least another two months before they would close the deal.

Sara had asked whether or not Jill could keep Chester that long. Jill had been about to explain the recent development with Mrs. Chatham when Sara had suggested that if Jill couldn't keep Chester, they could investigate the possibility of putting him in a kennel . . . as abhorrent as the idea was.

Chester in a kennel? The very idea of the little sweetheart penned in a kennel *was* unthinkable. Chester was hooked on the comforts of home. So she had assured Sara that of course keeping Chester wouldn't be an inconvenience.

Once the coffee was dripping, Jill settled behind her desk. She pulled open a drawer, lifted a map of Arizona from it and spread the map on the desk.

The first project on the agenda this morning was to begin making a list of possible places to schedule for day tours for the seniors. The tours would begin in January and although it was only October she wanted the schedule in place when the first of the snowbirds arrived in mid-November.

She and Shauna had broadly outlined their requirements. They were searching for places of interest that would require no more than three hours' driving time and could be offered for twenty dollars a person or less.

She was looking at the map when Shauna breezed into the office. "Mark my words," she said as she headed directly for the coffee. "Never again!"

Jill smiled. "I warned you. Never accept a blind date, not even one arranged by an acquaintance who attends the same church. And especially not if the date is a recently divorced brother. How bad was it?"

"He spent the evening talking about his ex," she said. She glanced at the desk, saw Jill didn't have her coffee and poured two cups. She carried them to the desk, set them down and pulled up a chair. "Toward ten—when I said that I had better get home—he began making remarks about how he *really missed the intimacy* of marriage."

Jill picked up her coffee, sipped. "I'll bet you had an answer for that."

"I wasn't polite in telling him I wasn't interested. All at once he was the one ready to go home," Shauna said. She half smiled. "Is there an abundance of divorced men on the prowl, or is it me? The last three guys I've dated were divorced men with nothing on their minds but *intimacy.*"

Jill thought of Steve. She'd met him a year ago when he joined the staff where she worked. Twice married, he had seemed on first impression to be egotistical. Then he began stopping in her office to talk, and she decided that he wasn't quite as self-centered as she'd first thought. Mostly, she decided, he was lonely.

She'd always had a soft spot for lonely people, a real need to ease their loneliness. To complicate matters she had been going through a "thirtysomething" identity crisis.

Her friends were married, starting families, and she suddenly had the awful feeling that she was missing something. So she accepted a dinner invitation from Steve, which led to a few more dates.

She was hoping that she might be falling in love with him when he started to press her to sleep with him. When she said no, he'd told her that she was hopelessly old-fashioned. How could *he* know whether or not they'd be sexually compatible if *he* didn't sleep with her.

That's when she got mad. At herself, mostly. He was exactly what she'd thought the first time she met him—so full of himself that he couldn't care about anyone else.

"You aren't alone when it comes to feeling that there is a scarcity of good men available," Jill said. She smiled. "You're twenty-three. Wait until you're as old as I am before you start to panic."

"I know your driver's license says you're thirty-three," Shauna said seriously, "but you look like a teenager."

"It's my height. No one takes anyone five foot four seriously. Mrs. Chatham doesn't, for sure," Jill said. She quickly filled Shauna in on the eviction notice.

"Mrs. Chatham sounds hard-hearted," Shauna offered, her brown eyes sympathetic. "The very idea. Evicting a pig."

"What about me?" Jill laughed. "She's putting me out, too."

"Oh, well. You, also," Shauna said. "What does your lease say about pets?"

"It specifies pets as a small dog or cat."

Shauna chuckled. "And when Chester walks like a pig and talks like a pig, it's hard to deny that he *is* a pig."

"Right."

"On the bright side, you want to move closer to the center," Shauna said.

"I intend to do just that, but the overhaul on my car last month depleted my savings," Jill said. "And knowing Mrs. Chatham, she'll hold my deposit on her place as long as she can. Any ideas, other than camping in my car?"

Shauna feigned deep thought. "Rob a bank," she said.

"I assume you're volunteering to drive the getaway car," Jill said.

"Sure," Shauna said. "But if you get caught, I'm telling the cop I was just parking when you came running from the bank, jumped into my car and ordered me to drive away."

"So much for robbing a bank," Jill said. "Guess I'll just have to think of something else." She pointed to the map. "Let's get down to the business of planning the tours."

"Okay," Shauna agreed, but before bending over the map she suggested, "Why not post a notice on the bulletin board that you're looking for a place to rent? One of the regulars might be looking for a tenant."

"Good thought, but there's still the matter of a deposit," Jill said. "And in this neighborhood the one hundred and fifty dollars I might be able to manage wouldn't get me a garage."

By the time Shauna left the office to prepare the tables for the morning bridge players, they'd compiled a list of twenty-odd possibilities for tours. They had also decided to ask the residents who lived in Mesa year-round for further day-tour suggestions.

Phone calls kept Jill busy for the next hour. She arranged for the Care car to pick up a woman whose husband was in a hospital; she explained the services the center provided to another, assuring her that she would be welcome, and invited her to visit. A man called to ask whether or not square dancing lessons would be scheduled. Jill informed him that Shauna was working on getting a sponsoring club. She took the man's name and address for the center's mailing list.

Between phone calls she scanned the advertisement section of the paper. She knew there was no way she could come up with the deposit on a house, so she concentrated on trailers. By circling only those that required a deposit of one hundred and fifty dollars or less, her search was drastically narrowed.

It was almost eleven when she left the office. The moment she stepped into the large social room, Belle Holiday beckoned her to the table where she was playing bridge with Ralph Iocker, Phoebe Tobias and Nell Tuttle.

Belle was slender, a strikingly beautiful gray-haired woman. She was easygoing, with a sense of humor. Belle was one of the seniors who not only patronized the center but worked as a volunteer. She drove the center's car, picking up seniors for trips to the doctor and shopping.

Only yesterday Jill had learned that Belle came from a farm southeast of Sioux City, Iowa, which was a skip away from Jill's hometown of Beaver Crossing.

She acknowledged Belle's beckoning with a wave, then weaved her way through the tables, speaking to the regular bridge players, introducing herself to several newcomers, asking if there was anything she could do for them.

"What's this we hear from Shauna about you being evicted because of Chester?" Belle asked when Jill reached the table.

"Mrs. Chatham gave me a choice. The house or Chester," Jill said. "I've decided to look for a trailer to rent."

"A trailer?" Phoebe asked. The woman's profile was cameo perfect, her hair short, worn with a fawn silver rinse. After her husband died she'd resumed her modeling career, doing shoots for clothing catalogs. "What's wrong with a house?"

"Nothing! I've...just always thought living in a trailer would be fun," Jill lied, trying to sound optimistic while she did it.

"Trailers cost too much to cool in the summer and too much to heat in the winter," Ralph stated. "You'd be better off with a house."

"Ralph is right," Belle said.

Jill felt as if she had been backed into a corner. "The truth is, I'm temporarily short on funds," she admitted. "I can swing a deposit on a trailer, but not a deposit on a house."

"I'll bet you can," Nell said. "Say three hundred—"

"Nell," Belle interjected, "if the girl can't come up with a deposit on a house, she can't be betting with you—"

"Who said anything about betting?" Nell asked.

"You did," Belle, Phoebe and Ralph said simultaneously before Belle concluded, "You said you'd bet she could—"

"Figure of speech," Nell huffed. She looked up at Jill. "I meant that I'll loan you the money. Three hundred. Five. Whatever."

Jill never ceased to wonder at the generosity of people, especially the seniors who had experienced rough times themselves. Nell and her husband, Herman, had lived in Wisconsin. They had purchased a small steak house when first married, lost it during the depression, but never lost sight of their dream. When Herman died, Nell sold the five steak houses they owned and operated.

Generous as Nell was, she was inclined to allow someone else to pay for her lunch. She never drove her town car if she could "hook a ride" and she constantly made small wagers on anything from who would come into the center the next time the door opened, to laying down two-dollar bets at the horse track.

"Thank you, Nell," Jill said. "But I couldn't do that."

Belle cleared her throat. "Ever since Shauna mentioned your dilemma, I've been thinking," she said. "Why don't you move in with me and my sons?"

"Excellent idea, Belle," Ralph said. "No sense in that lower-level apartment sitting idle."

"I couldn't move—" Jill was drowned out by Ralph, Nell and Phoebe asking in unison, "Why not?"

"Our house is large," Belle said. "The apartment Ralph mentioned is only used in January and February. That's when my sisters, their husbands and families visit. You're only looking for something for several months, aren't you?"

"Yes, but—"

"You know my husband and I were farmers," Belle stated. "I know something about pigs. A trailer court is no place for a pig. Not even a little pig."

"It would be an imposition," Jill said.

Belle met Jill's gaze. "It wouldn't be an imposition. I'm thinking of myself. I get lonely. Daniel is often gone and when he's home he spends most of his time in the workshop—"

"Is Daniel working on something now?" Nell asked.

"You know how Daniel is when he starts tinkering, as he calls it," Belle said. She bent, picked up her purse from the floor and took out a small notebook and a pencil. "He dwells in a world of his own. Nothing distracts him. Not even me. So . . . I'm sure that he is working on something, but as yet he hasn't told me what it is."

Phoebe and Ralph nodded as if in sympathy.

"Daniel needs a wife," Nell said.

"You're right," Phoebe said.

"If I was fifty years younger, maybe even twenty, I'd go after him myself," Nell said. When Ralph guffawed, she pivoted toward him. "You think that's funny, Ralph?"

"Hilarious, Nell," Ralph said. "Why turn a happy man into an unhappy one?"

"He's lonely, I tell you," Nell insisted.

"He's happy as a lark, tinkering," Ralph countered.

"All right, you two," Phoebe said. "Enough of the bickering. It's Daniel's life to live. By the way, Belle, I've been meaning to ask about Autry's Fountain Hill development. How is it going?"

Belle answered while drawing what appeared to be a map. "He's putting up twenty-five houses instead of the twenty he'd originally planned."

"Some people have the knack of turning everything they touch to gold," Ralph offered.

Nell made a tut-tut sound. "You'd better be on your toes when it comes to Autry, Belle," she advised. "There are a lot of gold diggers in this world. One of them might sneak up on him when he's not looking."

Belle laughed. "You know Autry doesn't need protecting," she said. "If he doesn't know all the angles, he's working on them."

She tore the sheet from the notebook and handed it to Jill. Jill glanced at the paper and saw that it was indeed a map.

"Go down Brown until it becomes Lost Dutchman Boulevard," Belle said. "Stay with the street until you come to Idaho Road. Turn left, go north. The map I've drawn should lead you right to us."

"I appreciate the offer, but—"

"A place for a couple of months. That's what you want and what I have to offer. Come out this evening. Look the place over," Belle said. "And bring Chester. I'm dying to meet the little fellow."

Daniel opened the refrigerator door, looking for the makings of a sandwich. His mother came from the family room.

"I'm on my way to the whirlpool," she said. "But I'd be happy to fix you something to eat."

Daniel grabbed some lunch meat, a jar of mayonnaise and a bottle of grape juice. He smiled at his mother as he set them on the counter. "I'm not that hungry. A sandwich and grape juice will hold me."

"At least you're taking time out to eat something," Belle said. "You don't take care of yourself, Daniel."

Daniel opened the bread drawer, removed a loaf and carried it to the counter. "I do. Light eating for a man my age is better than heavy. So...what went on at the center today?"

"Jill Fulbright has a problem—"

"Jill Fulbright?" Daniel asked. "Is she someone I should know?"

"You should," Belle said, gently reprimanding him. "I remember distinctly mentioning her on at least two occasions over the last three weeks."

"Three weeks?" Daniel asked. "I remember. The new administrator at the center!"

"You were guessing," Belle countered. "I'm renting the apartment to her."

"The apartment?" Daniel asked. He slapped the sandwich together. "Why?"

"Jill's being evicted at the end of the month because she has a pig."

"A pig?"

"A little potbellied pig," Belle said. She explained about Jill Fulbright's keeping Chester for some friends who were settling in Seattle, and about Mrs. Chatham's eviction notice. "So Jill needs a place to stay. It will be okay with you, won't it?"

"As long as she doesn't bother me, I don't care," Daniel said. "But what about the annual invasion?"

"Jill only needs temporary housing. She'll be gone by the time the family arrives."

"Fine," Daniel said. He quickly cleared the sandwich makings, took a glass from the cupboard for the juice. He was thinking about his latest project, an idea that had been bugging him for a long time. He was wondering whether—

"Daniel?" Belle asked.

"Yes?"

"Did you hear me tell you that Jill was coming this evening to look the place over?"

Daniel laughed. "Caught me. I'm sorry. She's coming this evening to look the place over. Does that have anything to do with me?"

"Would you like to meet her?"

Daniel shrugged his shoulders. "If she moves in, I'll meet her sooner or later."

"I do believe Autry is going to like Jill."

"Is she pretty?" Daniel asked.

"Oh, very," Belle said. "Tiny little thing with long blond hair, green eyes."

Daniel chuckled. "Then you know damn well my little brother will like her. Before I forget, Mother— got a call today that the boys have run into a few bugs with the new feeder. I'm going to fly back to Iowa on Monday. Would you care to go with me, spend a few days on the farm?"

"It sounds grand," Belle said. "The leaf color should be peaking right now. I'll think about it." She paused. "Jill is from Iowa. Beaver Crossing."

"That explains it," Daniel said. "Anyone from Iowa is family. That's what's behind your decision to help Jill Fulbright out."

"Do I need a reason?" Belle asked. She smiled serenely, fanned her hand through the air in a shooing manner. "Go. Get back to your work."

It was nearing sunset by the time Jill turned off Lost Dutchman Boulevard and headed north. Above, the undersides of the clouds were like a color chart ranging from gold to dark orange. Ahead, the mountains were shaded blues and grays.

She pulled over twice to check Belle's map. "I think we're on the right trail," she said, glancing at Chester, who was sitting in the passenger seat, riding on his haunches like a dog.

She made one last right turn and found herself on a road nearly free of traffic. When Belle said they lived in the country, she meant country. She was driving along what seemed to be a private paved road. The sequoia at the edge of the winding road loomed over her compact car. Once she spotted what she thought was a roadrunner, and several jackrabbits and rabbits.

The houses were large, sitting on acreages. Most had barns at the back of the acreage, and horses in pens. Three years in the valley and she'd never realized there was a place like this, secluded and quiet.

She reached a wrought-iron security gate. She slowed even though the gate was open, glancing up through the windshield to where a sign hung suspended by a chain. *Holiday.*

Right place, she thought. She looked up the driveway, past the desert landscaping to the house sitting close to the foothills of the mountains. It was Spanish in style, constructed in stucco, and there were so many pitches and angles in the tiled roof line it was difficult to determine how big the house was. But it was big . . . as in colossal.

If she hadn't made the commitment to show up tonight, she would have turned around. It was obvious that the environment was too rich for a working woman baby-sitting a pig.

She continued up the driveway, parking at the back of the house. She glanced around. Swimming pool. Tennis court. Two stucco buildings beyond them. She lifted Chester from the car, set him on the ground, then whistled for him to follow as she headed for the only door she saw, one set under a portico, near a six-stall garage attached to the house.

She rang the doorbell. Chimes sounded. She waited, listening for sound of movement in the house. Hearing nothing, she rang the bell again.

After a few minutes she stepped back, walked to the first garage door, raised to tiptoe. Three of the six stalls were empty, but Belle's large town car was there.

She walked back to the door, rang the doorbell again. How big was this house? she wondered. Big enough so that even if Belle heard the ring, it would take her five minutes to get to the door? She glanced back to the tennis court and swimming pool, to the two buildings beyond. No sign of life.

Who would see her if she walked off the length and width? she wondered. No one. Besides, there might be another entrance. Belle's car was here. Belle had to be inside.

"Let's go," she said to Chester, and strode away.

*   *   *

Daniel was in his workshop setting up an experiment with the old car he used for mountain driving when he heard a car drive in. When he didn't hear the garage door open, he walked to the shop window to see if one of Autry's friends had arrived early for the pool party Autry was having later.

Unless there was more than one woman with a pot-bellied pig, this had to be Miss Fulbright. She was petite, wearing a jumpsuit that looked as if it had been tie-dyed. The colors of spice and gold matched the highlights in her hair...but what the blue devil was she doing walking toward the end of the house in an awkward stride?

Woman and pig disappeared around the north end of the house. A few minutes later they returned. She stood, her hair billowing in the breeze while she tapped a meditative finger on her lip.

Daniel was wondering whether or not to step from the shop to tell her to go into the house when she took off again, throwing one spice-and-gold-covered leg as far forward as possible before striking out with the next. The little black pig, ears bouncing, trotted at her heels. What *was* she up to, he was wondering, when it came to him. She was measuring the length and width of the house! That's what she was doing.

He found her activity entertaining and annoying. He was entertained by her curiosity, annoyed thinking she might be impressed by the size of the house. And he didn't know why he should be annoyed. Most people were impressed by wealth.

But he wished he hadn't allowed Autry free rein in getting the house built. He'd asked Autry for something comfortable and hadn't taken into consideration what Autry would consider comfortable until the plans were drawn and they were studying them.

"Six thousand square feet, Autry! Give me a break," he'd said. "I asked for a house, not a damned hotel."

"Five thousand six hundred," Autry had corrected. "Not all that much space with three of us living there."

"I thought you and Crystal were talking about getting married," Daniel had said.

"Crystal who?" Autry had asked with a winning grin. "Now, about the house..."

Autry would marry someday. If not Crystal, then someone. In the end, Daniel had agreed to the size of the house because of the apartment. Daniel knew how important family was to his mother—especially important because she'd been without his father for so long. He still cringed when the memory cropped up unexpectedly. He turned from the window and walked back to the car.

Shelve the unpleasant memories, he told himself. And he could do that as soon as he got to work. He needed to repeat the experiment he had done last night. He picked up a spotlight. Miss Fulbright and her pig were forgotten.

Chapter Two

In Jill's journey around the house she had located three doors and had rung the bell at each. She had even—though she had felt like a sneak doing it—peeked into a window on the lower level, thinking she might see a light, some sign of life. All she'd seen in the darkened interior were the shadowy outlines of exercise equipment.

"I think we might as well leave," she said to Chester. "Belle must have forgotten we were coming. Someone must have picked her up."

She had opened the car door and was bent to scoop Chester up when her attention was drawn to one of the buildings beyond the swimming pool and tennis court. She was sure the building had been dark when she arrived. Now a light had been turned on.

Because the building was located farthest from the pool and tennis court and there was a driveway disappearing around it, she decided it had to be a maintenance building. It seemed unlikely, but Belle might be there.

"Let's investigate, shall we, Chester?" She shoved the car door shut and walked in the direction of the building. She passed the swimming pool, skirted the tennis court and approached the door. When she knocked, there was no response.

"This is the darnedest thing I've ever gotten into," she said. Chester snorted.

She raised to her toes to look through the door window. Shelves, tables, benches and tools. All the items one might find in a workshop. But there was also a desk, a telephone . . . a fax machine? A copier? And a computer? She found that unusual, to say the least.

At the far end of the building, close to double garage doors, a man was bent into the back seat of an older car. All she could see was a jean-covered posterior.

He appeared to be holding something. She lowered to her heels, knocked again, harder, then raised on her toes to check out his reaction. Not one indication he had heard.

Did she dare walk in? Darned right she dared. She was not being presumptuous. Even though she hadn't been able to raise Belle, it was difficult to believe that Belle had forgotten she was coming, so if Belle was around, the man might know where.

She opened the door. "Pardon me," she said. She stepped inside, working her way toward the car. "Pardon me," she said again.

She saw that what he was holding was a light of some kind, but if he had lost something and was looking for it, his method was strange. The beam of light stayed focused on one area.

"Pardon me," she said again. Still, absolutely no response. *What the heck,* she decided. She'd come this far. She might as well go the distance.

She stopped five feet from the car, standing at his back. Now in addition to his back and a head of dark hair, she could see his arms, elbows to hands. His fingers were long. He was on the slender side.

When he adjusted his hold on what she now saw was a spotlight, his shoulder muscles responded with a small ripple easily detected under the denim shirt he was wearing. Slender and muscular. Nice combination.

Personally, she was an eye person. The eyes told it all. She cleared her throat. "Ah . . . sir?"

When he still didn't respond, Jill assumed the man had a profound hearing loss. She moved to his left and presented herself at an angle where she felt he would see her.

It was definitely one of Belle's sons. The resemblance couldn't be missed. He had a good profile and strong cheekbones. His dark hair was wavy and slightly disheveled.

Suddenly he sensed she was present and glanced sideways at her, frowning slightly. Jill's breath caught. His eyes were exotic. Light blue, rimmed with black, framed with the longest, darkest lashes she had ever seen.

They were beautiful eyes, but it was what she saw in their depths that made her reflect that he was a gentle man.

This had to be Daniel, the tinkerer, not Autry, the gregarious. When she realized she had been staring, she said quickly, "I'm sorry if I startled you."

Startled was not one of the things Daniel had felt when he'd sensed someone had approached, and looked up. *She's younger than springtime,* he thought. He didn't feel guilty about paraphrasing the sentiment of the old song his mother liked to sing. It fit Miss Fulbright perfectly. Unblemished tanned skin, full lips, cheeks that rounded merrily when she smiled and eloquent, expressive green eyes.

"Sorry," he told her. "When I concentrate, I block out extraneous matter. If you knocked or called me, I simply didn't hear you."

"I've been called a lot of things, but never extraneous matter," she said.

He chuckled. Jill laughed. *What a marvelous smile!* he thought. "Is Mrs. Holiday home?" she asked.

"She is," he said. His voice was low and lively. "And presuming you're Miss Fulbright, she's expecting you."

"I am," Jill said. "But she hasn't answered the bell."

"She'd intended to take a whirlpool," he said amiably. "Perhaps she forgot the time. There's a sitting room off the kitchen. You might want to wait there."

In spite of his genial tone, it was obvious from the way his eyes kept drifting back to the car upholstery that he was eager to get back to doing whatever he was doing.

"Are you Daniel?" she asked.

"I'm Daniel," he said. He looked back to the spot where the beam of the spotlight was directed before touching the upholstery with his fingertips. "I should have introduced myself," he added without looking at her.

He was not *just* tinkering, Jill decided. But what the objective of holding a spotlight on the upholstery could be, she couldn't imagine. Whatever the objective, he was engrossed.

"Uh, Miss Fulbright," he said, glancing over his shoulder to meet her gaze, "your pig—"

"Chester."

"Chester is using my foot as a chair."

Jill hadn't seen Chester leave her side. Of course she hadn't—she'd been absorbed in the study of Daniel Holiday. She forced herself to look down.

Chester was indeed sitting on Daniel Holiday's foot, using it like a chair. She bent and picked him up. "I've never seen Chester do that before," she said. "Usually, he just rests his chin on a foot."

"Now you have," he said, "seen Chester *sit* on a foot."

His demeanor wasn't warm, nor was it cool. It was simply detached. He wanted to discourage further conversation.

Nevertheless, she found herself saying, "Mind telling me what you're doing?"

"With what?"

"The spotlight."

"Holding it."

His gaze came to her, warm and teasing. She chuckled nervously. "I'll be more specific. You're directing the beam at close range at one spot. The upholstery is going to get hot. So why are you doing it?"

"To see how hot it will get."

"Common sense tells me that if it gets hot enough it will burn."

"Common sense sometimes leads to erroneous conclusions."

Jill laughed. "Not this time," she stated.

No wonder his mother was eager to have Miss Fulbright as a renter, Daniel thought. Her energy sparkled through her eyes as brilliantly as stars sparkled on a cave-dark night.

Autry would go out of his mind with delight when he met her. "Whether or not it burns is immaterial," he said, ducking back into the car.

"How could burning the upholstery be immaterial?"

Daniel felt the upholstery. He was sure heat generated from a light bulb could be used as a power source. All he had to do was repeat the process of heating the upholstery and sooner or later it would come together. He would know exactly which step in experimentation should come next.

Ultimately, he would discover a way to use high, rapid heat on low amounts of energy. Down the line he envisioned a process that would heat homes and businesses without using gas or coal as energy sources. Something beyond the solar collectors—

A tap on his shoulder made him jerk his head around. He nearly bumped noses with Jill Fulbright, who had moved to peer over his shoulder. She was close enough for the scent of soap-freshened skin to drift to his nostrils. Close enough to be distracting.

Maybe she was not the twenty she looked, but she was young. He was forty, set in his ways. Over the years he had discovered there were a lot of things he liked, few that he didn't. One of the things he disliked was being distracted when he was trying to organize his thoughts.

He spoke gruffly. "This time you did manage to startle me, Miss Fulbright. I thought you'd taken your pig and gone."

"I don't think you're puttering—"

"Maybe I'm a touch crazy," Daniel suggested darkly.

She surprised him by laughing at his attempt to be sullen. "I'm sure of that, but please explain what you're doing," she said. "I mean ... if it wouldn't be too much trouble."

Because her voice sounded like the overflow of her laughter, and her eyes were bright with curiosity, he told her. "It's only a theory at this point," he said. "I think the heat generated from a light bulb can be used as a power source."

"Something like harnessing the sun's energy?"

"Something like that," he said. "I'm sure there is a way to develop high, rapid heat on low amounts of energy. Heat for such things as small tools like cordless hot glue guns, soldering irons and curling irons."

"Fascinating," she said. "But there are already cordless curling irons on the market. In fact, I have one."

With the natural curl of her hair, the easy way it danced on her shoulders, he wondered why she would curl it. "Do you find that it does a good job curling your hair?" he asked.

"You know," she said, pondering, "I had a curling iron that was heated by direct current and that iron did a relatively good job of curling my hair. But the cordless one doesn't. I rarely use it for that reason."

"Exactly. In order to curl hair, the temperature of the iron needs to be one hundred and twenty to one hundred and fifty degrees Centigrade," Daniel said enthusiastically. "If I'm right—" He suddenly realized he was getting carried away. "I'm sorry. I'm boring you."

"You aren't," she countered. "So ... what I'm seeing with the spotlight is the first step in the experimentation you hope will lead to an invention."

Daniel was smiling when he remembered how he had suggested to other women that he was boring them, how they denied he was, how he'd learned later that for one reason or another they'd lied. Likely, she was no different and he did not have time to play games.

"I'll repeat the heating of the upholstery," he said, sounding indifferent and strict. "Eventually the next step in experimentation will come to me. Providing I'm not distracted."

"It isn't my intent to distract you." Jill wondered what she had said to cause his smile to fade.

She started to turn away. But her gaze was on the spotlight beam, then on his long fingers moving over the upholstery. He was more interested in solving riddles of the mind than he was in her.

She should have been offended. After all, she was not above liking an approving glance, a verbal compliment. But she wasn't offended. Something told her that Daniel Holiday was—silly idea—afraid of her. Absurd as it was, she could not shake it.

"What do you think the next step will be?" she asked.

Daniel looked at her. She was looking at the yellow-white circle of the spotlight on the upholstery. "I don't have the vaguest idea at this point," he said.

Chester grunted as Jill shifted him in her arms. "But you do have an idea of how it might be done."

She *was* persistent. "It might be done by using reflected light, a prism. I don't know right now," he said.

"Thank you for satisfying my curiosity," she said.

When she turned to leave, Daniel knew he should let it rest, but he couldn't. "Before you go, satisfy *my* curiosity," he said. "How many square feet did you decide were in the house?"

"How did you know I was measuring the house?" she asked.

Smile power, he reflected. That's what she had. Smile power. "Anyone who grew up on a farm or in a farming community knows the stride used to get a rough measurement," Daniel said.

"Approximately five thousand square feet," she said. "With the garage and all the angles of the house, it was a tough measure."

"Five thousand six hundred," Daniel said. "Are you impressed?"

"Of course I'm impressed," she said. "Wouldn't you be, if you were seeing the house and grounds for the first time?"

"Youth is sometimes easily impressed," Daniel said.

"Did you intend that to be some cryptic speculation on my personality?" she asked.

"So intended," he admitted.

"Then allow me to give you the correct perception. I'm not easily overwhelmed," she retorted. "Nor am I that young."

"I've been properly chastised and corrected," he said. "I would like to get back to work, if you don't mind."

"I apologize for interrupting," she said.

"No apology needed, Miss Fulbright," he said. "As long as it doesn't routinely happen after you move in."

"I never go where I'm not wanted," she stated, then turned away.

Daniel knew he'd hurt her feelings but the door had closed behind her before he'd reached a decision about what to do about it. On the one hand, she had interrupted. She had infringed on his privacy.

On the other hand, she had a legitimate reason. She'd been looking for his mother. He could have been more tactful when he told her that when he was working he didn't appreciate interruptions by anyone. Instead, he'd made it sound as if he considered her interruption an intrusion and was singling her out for reprimand.

Why he'd done it he didn't fully understand, but he thought it was because he had found himself attracted to her. He simply did not know how to handle himself when it came to a woman. Especially one who had stimulated his interest as she had...

The bottom line was that he had been deliberately rude to Jill Fulbright and he did owe her an apology.

Jill did not often draw inaccurate conclusions about people. But she wondered if she hadn't jumped too quickly to the conclusion that Daniel Holiday was a sensitive man. He probably was exactly what his actions depicted—surly and cool.

She was muttering to Chester as she closed the door. "I'll tell you one thing. If he is as gruff with Belle's friends as he was with me, no wonder she gets nods of sympathy from them."

"Jill! Here I am, dear," Belle called from where she stood under the portico at the back door. "Daniel didn't toss you out, did he?"

Jill set Chester on the ground and walked to join Belle. "I think so," she said.

Belle was wearing light yellow crinkled-cotton slacks and matching jersey. She bent, rubbed Chester behind the ears, laughing up at Jill. "Ignore Daniel when he acts that way," she said.

"Daniel is hard to ignore," Jill observed. "He's rather overpowering."

Belle pressed her lips to an O. She asked in perfect high-pitched mimic of a sex counselor on a weekly television series," Really? Overpowering, dear? Want to tell me how? Sexually, maybe?"

"No," Jill sputtered through her laughter.

"Too bad, dear," Belle said, using the same high-pitched voice. She rolled her eyes. "Maybe another time."

"Belle! That's marvelous. Shauna's arranging an amateur talent night. You'll have to volunteer to do that impression."

"People think I'm a dignified woman," Belle said. "I wouldn't want to blow my image." She laughed. "But how did you find Daniel overpowering?"

There were a few reactions to Daniel that Jill wouldn't confide in her own mother, let alone Belle. Those that had been sensual in nature, like the soaring sensation she'd felt looking into his eyes...

"This is going to sound silly, but I felt as if he were treating me like a child," Jill said. "Not as an adult. Foolish. Right?"

"I'm sure Daniel didn't view you as a child, but he may well have given you that impression," Belle said. She sighed. "Daniel never had—" she paused to consider her words "—what most people would consider a normal childhood. His father died when he was twelve, Autry five. For various reasons, Daniel assumed the role of man in the family."

"So Daniel is the eldest?" Jill asked.

"Yes, he is," Belle said.

"The oldest child often assumes the role of mother or father when a death occurs," Jill offered.

"Indeed they do," Belle agreed. "The problem with Daniel is that he assumes responsibilities he shouldn't feel obligated to assume. But enough of that. Let's take a look at the apartment."

Belle slipped her arm through Jill's. She pulled her along the east side of the house to where the sidewalk circled down an incline to the lower level.

"I don't think this is the place for Chester and me—"

"How do you know?"

"My goodness," Jill said, laughing. "I don't have to see the inside of the house to know this isn't exactly the place for a pig."

"Did Daniel say something to make you think he objected to having you here?"

Jill smiled. Other than *don't make a habit of invading my space?* "Daniel didn't say anything," she said. "It's my impression. By no stretch of imagination can I see Chester romping around this place."

"It is downright ostentatious," Belle stated. She laughed. "But when Autry had the plans drawn, he was thinking about what he and Daniel call the annual invasion of the family. Now we have room enough to accommodate everyone who comes and we don't have to draw numbers to get into a bathroom."

Jill chuckled. "You enjoy having your family around, don't you?"

"I certainly do," Belle said. "And the boys do, also. Autry especially. He's gregarious. The more, the merrier, you know. I'm positive you'll like Autry."

The apartment door was protected by a red-tiled portal. Belle dropped Jill's arm, opened the door and stepped inside. Jill scooped up Chester and stepped into the atrium.

Beyond, the Spanish motif of the exterior had been carried into the front room, which was large enough to be a hotel waiting room, complete with fireplace and brightly colored rugs scattered over the redbrick tile floor. There were four sofas and numerous chairs.

The wall of windows facing south was shaded by the second-story balcony. Belle opened the drapes to reveal the landscape, a pattern of desert, valley and the Superstition Mountains to the southeast.

Chester wriggled. Jill adjusted her hold, crooned soothingly.

"Put Chester down," Belle suggested.

"I don't know, Belle," Jill said. "He's housebroken but I wouldn't want to test him in this room."

"Nonsense. He's uncomfortable being held." Belle took Chester from Jill's arms, scratched him behind the ears. "He's a cute little fellow," she said. She set him down. "This way to the kitchen."

Jill followed Belle. Chester followed Jill. The kitchen-dining area was one with twelve chairs around a glass-topped table. The kitchen was made for a gourmet, which Jill wasn't.

The three bedrooms were beautifully finished, each with a king-sized bed. In the master bedroom Belle opened the doors to a walk-in closet that was as big as Jill's present bedroom. If she had saved all the clothes she had ever owned, she couldn't begin to fill the racks and shelves.

The bath held tub, shower and whirlpool. There was a separate vanity and powder room. When they were in the laundry room, Belle pointed to a closed door. "Behind that door is an exercise room and the sauna. Of course, you're welcome to use them."

"It's tempting," Jill said. "But—"

"I thought we'd agreed not to discuss it until the tour is ended," Belle said firmly. "By the way, is your house furnished?"

"Yes," Jill said.

"Good. Then moving won't be too difficult, will it? Just your personal possessions."

Dollar signs flashed before Jill. "You're renting this apartment furnished?"

"Of course," Belle said. "What would we do with all the furniture if we didn't rent the apartment furnished?"

Jill laughed. "You could start a furniture store."

"Or have a garage sale. I love garage sales," Belle said. "And flea markets."

"Me, too," Jill said. "I think I'm going to limit myself to the purchase of one or two books, and come home with half a dozen."

"If you like to read, you'll love Daniel's library. It's upstairs, off the den," Belle said. "You may as well take advantage of it while you're here. And maybe you and I could sneak off to the flea markets from time to time."

"Belle," Jill said firmly. "I can't afford to live in a place like this. The electric bill alone would eat up my paycheck."

"Let's go sit by the pool and discuss it," Belle suggested.

Jill sighed. She had not guessed Belle would be so determined. Did she feel sorry for Jill? Or was she really lonely?

At the pool they settled on Hampton chairs, made comfortable by pillowed seats and backrests. The view from here, as it had been in the apartment, was magnificent. In the near valley only a sprinkling of lights was visible, while the undersides of the clouds reflected the last rays of red sunset and the collective lights of Mesa and Scottsdale.

"I do love the silence out here," Jill said.

Belle smiled. "I enjoy living in Arizona. And for the most part it is quiet here. Still, I miss the special kind of quiet on the farm early in the morning."

Jill nodded. "The crack-of-dawn quiet," she said. "I miss that, too. And the smell of the grass and trees after a rain."

"Mind if I join you?" Daniel asked.

Jill didn't know whether she was surprised or pleased to see him. *Pleased,* she thought. Then as he circled his mother's chair, carrying a tray with three tall glasses of iced tea, that thought was waylaid by another. He was limping. Noticeably. She hadn't noticed it earlier. Had he pulled a muscle?

He set the tray on the table between Jill and Belle, then handed a glass to Jill. "Peace offering," he said before taking a glass for himself and settling into the chair next to her.

"A peace offering isn't necessary," Jill said. "You didn't actually declare war on me."

"I apologize for being rude," he said.

Jill loved the glimmer of humor in his eyes. It made him approachable. "I'll accept the apology," she said slowly. She traced a trail of moisture forming on the tall glass with her fingers before meeting his gaze again. "Because you were *very* rude."

"I wasn't *very* rude."

"You probably were, my dear," Belle put in.

Daniel laughed, leaning forward to look past Jill. "If you aren't going to defend me, Mother," he said, "please stay out of it. Miss Fulbright is capable of defending herself."

"I did ask him questions while he was trying to concentrate," Jill offered.

"She did do that, Mother," Daniel agreed. "She hung around—"

"I did not hang around!"

Belle chuckled. "I'm happy to see the two of you getting along so well," she said.

Jill went through the motions of laughing, smiling and exchanging small talk, but her mind was locked on Daniel's proximity to her. He'd showered and shaved, and smelled lightly of spice cologne. He was wearing light blue casual slacks and a light blue golf shirt. He looked wonderful in that color.

"So you miss the smell of Iowa rain, Miss Fulbright," he said. Chester left Jill's feet to sit at Daniel's. Daniel leaned forward, rubbed the pig behind the ears, then leaned back again.

"Yes," she said. "Especially the smell of a spring rain."

"Nothing smells quite like a spring rain in Iowa. If someone could package that, it would make a million," he said.

"Daniel," Belle said. She sighed for dramatic, teasing effect. "How many times must I suggest that not everything in life should be judged on the basis of its material value?"

"Mother is only pretending to tease," Daniel informed Jill. "She's actually lecturing me."

Belle smiled affectionately at Daniel. "Perhaps I would stop if you'd listen to me."

Daniel chided Belle with a gentle laugh. "How old do you think a man has to be before his mother stops giving him advice, Miss Fulbright?"

The exchange between Daniel and Belle was the first indication Jill had had that not all the money in the family was being made by Autry. Coupled with Belle's earlier observations about Daniel's childhood, she began to suspect that she had guessed right. There was more to Daniel's tinkering than simply plain old everyday tinkering.

"I don't know how old a man has to be before his mother stops giving him advice," Jill said. "But if your mother believes you're still in need of guidance, I wouldn't question her judgment."

Chapter Three

Daniel feigned affront while his mother chuckled.

"I believe I need a sour cream cookie with my tea," Belle said. "Do either of you want one?"

"No, thank you," Jill said.

"I don't think so," Daniel said.

"I'll bet Chester would like a cookie," Belle said.

Jill laughed. "He would, but he's only allowed sweets in a small amount."

"I'll be back in a jiffy," Belle said and hurried away.

After Belle had gone, Daniel said, "I should have guessed you wouldn't pull any punches in giving your opinion."

Jill thought it went beyond guessing. He had been evaluating her from the moment they met. She'd seen him reflect upon every glance she offered, the inflection of her voice when she spoke. It was almost as if he did not trust what he saw, so he was searching for the truth beneath it.

"I always try to be honest," she said.

"Even when you know an honest opinion is going to hurt?" he asked.

"Even then," Jill said.

"I admire that quality," he said thoughtfully.

Jill drank the last of her tea, glanced to the sky. "Aren't you always honest?" she asked.

He came forward in the chair, placing his elbows on his knees and rolling his glass between his hands. "I'm always candid when it comes to business," he said.

Jill noted how he had phrased his answer. *Candid when it comes to business.* She believed when it came to personal relationships he would probably avoid giving an opinion if he knew that opinion was going to offend.

He dropped one hand and scratched Chester behind the ear. Chester's snoring momentarily ceased, recommencing when Daniel stopped scratching.

"I understand your hometown is Beaver Crossing," he said. "I've been through it. A lovely little town nestled in the base of the bluffs." He closed his eyes.

Jill chuckled. "Don't tell me the conversation is so boring you've decided to take a catnap."

He laughed. "I'm trying to visualize a sign I saw near the south edge of town."

"Really?"

"Really," Daniel said. He did concentrate on the sign but before he could bring it into focus, the image of Jill Fulbright, all five foot four of her, materialized, even to her hair rippling in the breeze. He felt her studying him, wondered what she was thinking...and wondered at himself that he cared what she thought.

He opened his eyes. "The sign says Beaver Crossing. The Farthest West Is The Best. Population 503."

"That's right," she agreed. "When were you there?"

"The year the annual bike ride across Iowa started in Akron."

"That was fourteen years ago!" she said. "Because the ride started in a town so close to us, I talked my cousin and two friends into making the trip. They still hound me about the week of self-inflicted pain."

Daniel laughed. "I talked Autry into going with me. Midday of the first day out he dropped off the pace, wangled a ride with a pretty girl from Des Moines who was driving one of the escort cars. That was the last I saw of my gregarious brother."

Jill doubted that Autry's desertion had meant Daniel had ridden alone. There had been fifteen hundred riders on the trip—a riot of pretty young women biking across Iowa that year. Daniel was probably lucky to have survived the stampede in his direction.

"I'm back," Belle announced. She set a plate filled with cookies on the table, then eased down into the chair. "Daniel. Do you know Jill's lived in the valley six years?"

"Six years?" Daniel asked. He reached for a cookie and looked at Jill. "How much can Chester have?"

"Half will be enough. In small pieces," she said, smiling. "Just wave it under his nose. That will wake him."

Daniel broke off a small piece and leaned down. Chester woke with a snort, stood, stretched like a dog, then rose to his hind legs. Before Daniel could slip the cookie to him, he made a three-hundred-and-sixty-degree turn.

"Good grief," Daniel said. He and Belle laughed when, between each piece, the little pig did a dance.

When the cookie was gone, Belle asked, "Did you teach Chester to do that?"

"No," Jill said. "His owners told me that he taught himself. I've seen him spin until he actually gets dizzy."

Daniel reached down, scratched Chester behind the ear. Chester, in return, used Daniel's leg as a scratching post, pressing into it, moving blissfully back and forth.

"In six years Jill's never been to places like Sedona, Oak Creek Canyon or Arcosanti," Belle said, returning to the earlier conversation. "Can you believe that, Daniel?"

Daniel glanced at Jill. She was looking at his mother, puzzled. Belle looked meaningfully at him. He didn't have the vaguest idea what his mother wanted him to say.

"Ah...so you haven't visited the tourist attractions," he said, feeling stupid.

"I did visit the south rim of the Grand Canyon," Jill said. "But it's true that I haven't seen a lot of the country. It seemed that whenever I planned to take a day to play tourist, something came up with one of my people—"

"Your people?"

"I was a social worker," she said. "I had a rather heavy caseload and problems weren't limited to weekdays."

"I heard you and Shauna talking about camping," Belle said. "You love to camp, don't you?"

"Yes, I—"

"Daniel," Belle said. "Maybe you and Autry will take her along some weekend when you're going up to the cabin." She looked to Jill. "They have a lovely place near Sedona."

What in the hell was his mother doing? Daniel wondered. Autry's idea of roughing it was having his golf ball land in the sand trap on the sixteenth green—Autry seldom used the cabin.

It finally dawned on Jill that Belle had assumed she was going to rent the apartment. "That's a generous offer, Belle," she said. "But I won't be here because I'm not going to rent the apartment. Chester and I wouldn't fit in here."

"We're not stodgy people," Belle said. "If Daniel has no objections to Chester's being here, you shouldn't."

"Belle," Jill said, gently but firmly, "the truth is, I can't afford it."

"How do you know you can't afford it?" Belle asked. "We haven't discussed what we're asking. Daniel, what do you think would be fair? A few hundred a month? Utilities included?"

Daniel shrugged. He had absolutely no idea what the going rate for an apartment might be. But he was beginning to fully understand that it was immaterial. His mother was set on having Jill Fulbright around. As for himself, he had no preferences, one way or another. He would seldom see her.

"That sounds fair to me," he agreed. "But you might want to check with Autry."

"I don't think we need to do that," Belle said. "Is that agreeable, Jill?"

"That would be more than fair, but—"

"Of course you'll need a pen for Chester," Belle said. "Daniel has to leave for Iowa on Monday. He'll be gone for several days, but I'm sure that when he gets back he'll come up with something for Chester. Won't you, dear?"

"Oh. Sure," Daniel agreed, as if what he really wanted to do when he got back from Iowa was build a pigpen.

In the end, Jill Fulbright agreed to be the Holiday's renter for the months of November and December.

"I'm glad that's settled," Belle said. "Now what about moving? Do you have someone to help you? Autry—"

"I can handle moving myself by doing a bit every night after work," Jill said, not quite believing she had been skillfully outmaneuvered by Belle into agreeing to rent the apartment.

"You'll need keys to the gate and the house," Belle said. "I'll go get the extra set now before I forget about it."

She stood and took one step toward the house. "I see cars coming up the drive," she said. "It looks as if Autry and his friends are arriving for their pool party." She glanced back at Jill, smiling. "This is the end of the quiet. But I'm glad Autry arrived before you left. I wanted you to meet him."

With that, realization came to Daniel like the proverbial flash. *That* was why his mother had been so uncharacteristically persistent. She was hoping Jill and Autry would hit it off.

"My goodness," Jill murmured as Belle hurried away. "I would never have guessed she would be...well...so determined."

Daniel chuckled. "I've never seen her use bulldozer tactics before," he said. "And she did roll over you, didn't she?"

She met his gaze, held it. "Is my renting the apartment going to inconvenience you, personally?"

Daniel shifted, set his glass aside. A lot of thoughts had occurred to him regarding her. Inconvenience had not been one of them. "In spite of my conduct earlier," he said slowly, "I assure you, you won't bother me at all."

Well, Jill thought. She hadn't expected anything like *Oh, I'll love having you here,* but she hadn't expected anything so brusque as *you won't bother me at all.*

She glanced over her shoulder. Five cars had parked in the driveway, and perhaps twenty people were standing in couples or small groups, talking. Belle hadn't made it to the house yet. She floated from one group to another.

A young man wearing a broad smile broke from a group visiting with Belle and headed straight for them.

Jill drank the last of her iced tea and set the glass on the tray. "I should be going," she said.

"Stay a minute. Autry's on his way over," Daniel said. "I knew it wouldn't take him long to seek out an attractive new face."

Jill was flattered by the offhand compliment—what woman wouldn't feel delighted to hear Daniel express the opinion that she was attractive. On the other hand, he had sounded like a benevolent father, proud of a son's prowess.

"Daniel, you old devil," Autry said. His smile broadened. "What's holding up the official introduction?"

"Miss Fulbright—my brother, Autry."

Autry extended his hand. "Hello, Jill Fulbright. Mother tells me that we're renting the apartment to you."

Dark haired like Daniel, Jill appraised as they shook hands. Handsome like Daniel, but unlike Daniel, Autry was cocky. Easy to like, she decided, but difficult to take seriously.

"Hello, Autry," she said.

"Has anyone ever told you that you're gorgeous?"

Because Autry seemed to have no intention of giving her hand back, Jill withdrew it, smiling up at him as she did. "Phoebe and Nell have informed me that your opening line to every woman you meet, no matter the age, is to tell her that she's gorgeous."

"Leave it to Nell and Phoebe to extol my virtues," Autry said. With the grace of a large cat, he settled on the chair his mother had vacated and appraised Chester. "I thought I'd seen the last of pigs."

"You don't like pigs?" Jill asked.

"It's more like I was not particularly fond of the work that went with them when we were still on the farm," Autry said.

"If you don't like the idea of having Chester around—"

"No problem," Autry interjected. "I like the idea of having you around." He beamed. "You really are beautiful. I think I'm in love. Want to marry me?"

Autry played the rascal role to its fullest. Jill was enjoying his banter until she became aware that Daniel seemed to be enjoying it even more.

It was no concern of hers, she assured herself, if Daniel seemed to glow with affection for his younger brother. What bothered her was his willingness to defer to Autry. It was almost as if he expected her to prefer Autry's company over his.

"Want to marry you?" she asked, smiling at Autry. "Why not? I don't have anything else planned for the next ten minutes."

"Little lady, you and I are going to get along great."

The first of Autry's guests arrived at poolside, tossed towels to chairs in preparation for swimming. Still others meandered toward the bathhouse. Autry made a flurry of introductions.

When two younger women arrived, Autry introduced them as Margaret and Joanna. Each was tall and long legged—real beauties, Jill thought.

She smiled. "Meet Chester," she said.

Chester was awakened, tickled behind the ears and had his nose tapped by the pair. When Daniel broke off another small piece of cookie and Chester demonstrated his dancing ability, they laughed.

Jill knew the two women were entertained by Chester's antics, but their real interest was in Daniel. Time and again, Margaret and Joanna's gazes drifted to him, sultry and suggestive.

She wasn't mistaken in what she was seeing. After all, limited as her love life had been, she had gazed longingly at a man a few times...and on occasion had gotten more action in return than she had really wanted.

However, Daniel's reaction to their attention was almost indifferent. *He probably has more women on the line than he can handle,* she decided.

When Margaret and Joanna drifted away, Autry stood and hovered over Jill. "There are extra suits in the bathhouse. Will you join us for a swim? We'll be having steaks later."

"Thank you anyway, but I've already eaten," Jill said. "And I never learned to swim."

"That's no problem," Autry said. "I'll teach you. Swimming is just like dancing—you do dance?"

"Oh, yes," Jill said. "I dance."

"Well, swimming is like dancing, only better," Autry said rakishly, "because it's sensuous."

"Sensuous sounds good," Jill said. "And it truly breaks my heart but I really can't stay because it's Chester's bedtime."

Autry groaned. "I've been turned down by a woman going home to tuck a pig in bed. If something like that got out it would tarnish my reputation."

"Rest easy, Autry," Jill assured him soberly. "Your tarnished reputation is safe with me."

Autry slapped his head lightly. "I do really believe I'm in love."

Laughing, Jill stood, snapped her fingers. Chester's head came up. He rose and trotted to her. She turned to Daniel. "Good night, Mr. Holiday. Thank you for the tea."

"Daniel," he offered.

Jill warmed. Autry had assumed a first-name basis, which was fine, but Daniel's offer told her she had gained a measure of respect from him. "Good night, Daniel."

"I'll walk you to the car," he said.

"I'm up," Autry said. "I'll walk her."

Jill wanted to decline and accept Daniel's offer, but Autry had already slipped his hand to her elbow. She whistled for Chester to follow.

Daniel watched Jill and Autry walk toward her car. Jill Fulbright was exactly what his brother needed, a gentle but firm hand. In a way, she was a lot like Autry, also. She had easily exchanged a few words with each of the guests Autry had introduced. And she had charmed Margaret and Joanna, who, in his opinion, were the least likable of Autry's friends.

Yes, he decided. The rapport he had expected to develop between Jill and Autry had developed. He had vicariously enjoyed it even though he had begun to feel ill at ease the moment Autry's friends had arrived.

It was not that he didn't like them. It was only that he had nothing in common with them. Maybe he *was* stodgy. He swam laps because it was good for him, therefore not a waste of time. But he considered sitting around at a pool party chatting between dives a waste of good time.

As he stood to go back to his work, Belle came from the house and joined Autry and Jill, giving Jill the key to the gate and apartment. He watched Jill and Chester get into the car as his mother went back into the house. Autry lingered at the window on the driver's side, talking with Jill.

Daniel's mind shifted gears. He knew what he needed to do next in his experiment. As he walked toward his workshop, he couldn't help glancing toward the drive. Autry was still talking to Jill. Odds were Autry would talk her into staying.

He had arranged a battery and a soldering iron on one of the worktables. He was reaching to plug in the soldering iron when Autry threw the door open.

"Marian Babbitt just arrived," he said as he strode toward Daniel.

"Marian Babbitt?" Daniel wondered.

"I told you about Marian," Autry said. "Neat gal. Kind of quiet. Recently widowed. Two kids. She's purchased a home in the Fountain Hills development."

"I remember," Daniel said. He plugged in the soldering iron. "Marian Babbitt. Blond. Forty—"

Laughing, Autry jerked the cord out. "You don't remember one thing I told you. Marian has black hair, brown eyes. And I asked whether or not it was okay with you if I invited her out tonight because I wanted you to meet her.''

"What did I say?" Daniel asked, about to plug in the soldering iron.

Autry halted his hand. "You know you said okay or she wouldn't be here. And if you start working, by the time you get back outside the party will be long over. You know it, buddy."

"Tell you what," Daniel said. "Give me a half hour alone and I promise I will come out and meet—ah—what did you say her name was?"

Autry shook his head, laughing. "You're impossible. Marian. Marian. Marian. Got it?"

"Got it," Daniel said. "By the way, did you talk Jill into staying?"

"Talked until I was blue in the face and she still left to put Chester to bed," Autry said. He laughed. "Fun lady, isn't she?"

Daniel thought Jill Fulbright was more than just a *fun* lady. "She's that," he agreed. "Perceptive, also."

"Perceptive?"

Daniel quickly told Autry about Jill's walking in when he was holding the spotlight. "She grasped the basic premise of what I was doing right away," he ended.

"Good Lord." Autry chuckled. "Am I going to have to live with two blooming geniuses?"

"Get out of here," Daniel said. He tossed his head in the direction of the door. "Or I'll never get around to meeting—what the devil was the woman's name?"

"Marian," Autry said. He walked toward the door, paused as he opened it. "By the way, Jill said she was going to start moving her books over here tomorrow. She must have a bunch of them. You've got something else in common. Now, don't forget—"

"Marian!"

Laughing, Autry left.

Long after his brother had gone, Daniel pondered their conversation. He could take lessons from Autry when it came to women. But why did Autry have to pick someone quiet? Someone widowed? Someone with kids? Did even his brother consider him dull?

Maybe so. His relationship with women—he had had four relationships if he counted every one from Patti, a high school girl who'd had a fifteen-minute crush on him, to Christina . . .

Ah, yes, he thought. Christina. She had summed him up best when she'd said, "At first I found your good looks and eccentricity exciting. I don't anymore. I want a man who will concentrate on *me* when I'm with him, not on his next experiment. Frankly, Daniel, you are a pain in the you-know-where."

Even then, Christina had not been entirely honest, he reflected sarcastically. Honesty would have demanded that she admit that what she'd found attractive at first had been his money. . . .

Once he had worried about whether or not people liked him, or approved of him, or loved him. He didn't do that anymore. Early in life he had learned a disheartening lesson about human nature. The more effort he put into trying to gain approval, the more likely he was to be rejected.

His father's rejection, no matter how he tried to analyze it, had hurt worst of all.

Chapter Four

Jill started scrambling at seven the following morning. After attending church at nine, she stopped at a grocery store in a nearby mall and picked up a load of cardboard boxes.

She changed clothes, fed Chester and then began packing the books she had stored in the kitchen cupboards. In the front room she had constructed a bookcase of boards and bricks. It wasn't pretty—a carpenter she wasn't—but it was functional. The bookcase was also loaded.

Her thoughts flew to the spacious master bedroom at the Holiday house, and to the shelves in the walk-in closet next to it.

The closet would make a perfect library. It might be foolish to go to all the work of unpacking her books for such a short stay, but that was exactly what she intended to do.

The vision of having her books lined on shelves that didn't threaten to topple was enough to cause her to flip on the radio and sing while she worked. Before one o'clock she had loaded the back seat and trunk of the car. With luck she would manage two, maybe three, trips today and that would take care of the books.

She'd seen Chester observing her as she dashed about, watching carefully each time she headed for the door. Now, as she grabbed her purse from the sofa, he interpreted it as a signal that he might be in for a ride, so he trotted after her.

"I'm afraid it's too hot for you to ride along this trip, Chester," she said. "But I promise you can go along the next time. Okay?"

Chester grunted and trotted, ears flopping, for the bedroom. "I'm sounding like Harriet," Jill muttered as she closed the door and locked it.

Harriet Hoover was a seventy-year-old woman who lived in Beaver Crossing. Eight years ago Clinton Hoover had run off with a woman half Harriet's age. After Clinton left, Harriet started talking to herself. Occasionally, she was overheard describing the more intimate details of her marriage in graphic detail. While most people felt sorry for Harriet, that didn't keep them from listening.

Jill's relationship with Stephen had not been long-standing, and sexually, it didn't hold a candle to Harriet's revelations.

In the end, Stephen hadn't driven her to talking to herself. He hadn't even driven her to the point where she distrusted men. She had, however, resolved not to allow the desire to marry and have children to lead her into misreading her emotions again.

She slipped the key into her purse, glancing toward Mrs. Chatham's house in time to see the curtain fall. Jill had never met a person she didn't like, but Mrs. Chatham came close. For as long as Jill had lived in the house, Mrs. Chatham had hidden behind that curtain, snooping.

The curtain fluttered again. Jill smiled toward the window, waved and called, "What I'm doing is moving, Mrs. Chatham."

Daniel was not going to the window to see whether or not it was Jill who'd driven in. He knew it had to be. His mother was having dinner with Phoebe, Ralph and Nell. Autry was playing golf.

He was going to the window, he told himself, simply to confirm that it was Jill. Then he would get back to work. Sure, he was curious. At breakfast he'd tuned in when Autry had swung the conversation to Jill. In particular, Autry had wanted to know whether or not she was dating anyone special.

His mother didn't know. She'd added, "But I don't think so. Jill's been at the center for three weeks. I'm sure if there was someone in her life, we'd have seen him by now."

"And Nell and Ralph would be on the alert, wouldn't they?" Autry had said. "So there's no visible man in our Miss Fulbright's life."

Daniel had laughed. "Better watch yourself, Autry. I think Mother's caught the matchmaking bug from Phoebe and Nell."

"Mother!" Autry had teased. "You wouldn't do that to me, would you?"

Belle had chuckled. "You know me better than that," she'd said. "But I do think Jill will make some man a wonderful wife, don't you?"

Daniel arrived at the window in time to see Jill lift a box of books from the trunk of the car. She was wearing a body-clinging knit pantsuit blossoming with red and yellow flowers and green leaves. The top was a draped, twisted bandeau that bared her tanned shoulders. The pants were held at her waist by a drawstring.

She started down the sidewalk. When the weight of the box caused her to run down the slope, rather than walk, Daniel was immediately apprehensive. If she turned her ankle, she could break a leg.

He glanced at the battery and soldering iron he'd placed on the worktable, then back to her car. From the looks of it, the back seat was also loaded with boxes.

"Nuts," he muttered. He walked to the soldering iron, unplugged it and headed toward the door.

She was coming up the walk as he was going down with a box of books. "You didn't have to do that," she said.

The smile in her eyes was as sensitive as he'd remembered. And better to concentrate on the slight slant of her eyes than her bare, silky-skinned shoulders.

"I don't do anything I don't want to do," he said. "Where's Chester?"

"Home. Never?"

"All right. Sometimes I do things I'd rather not do," Daniel conceded.

"Like helping me with the books when you'd rather be working on your experiment," she said, rushing on before Daniel could reply. "You know I put the boxes into the car, so I'm capable of taking them out. You don't need to help."

"We're wasting time arguing," he said. When he continued walking, she raced to the apartment and opened the door. "Listen," he said as he passed through, "I'm helping you, not doing all the lugging while you open and shut the door."

"Oh, I intend to help carry," she said. "But I noticed that your leg is giving you more trouble today than it did last night. If you strain an already pulled muscle, you'll cause further injury. I don't want you to do that on my account. So I'm holding the door."

Daniel's thoughts flashed back to the day he and his father were unloading ear corn from a wagon into an elevator that would carry it to be dropped into the corncrib. The wagon was almost unloaded and his father had climbed into it to rake the corn toward the gate. Autry was playing nearby.

Daniel was picking up corn that had overshot the elevator, looking forward to quitting time. He was making a unicycle in the shop and couldn't wait to get back to it. He was thinking about that when his father yelled.

Daniel looked up to discover that Autry had climbed onto the elevator. In Daniel's haste to turn off the tractor, instead of climbing to the seat, he had tried to reach the key by stepping on the drawbar.

He could still feel his jeans catching in the power take-off, feel the pain sear his body. He could still hear his father screaming, "Dammit! Look what your daydreaming got you!"

"It isn't a pulled muscle," he told Jill now. "I was caught in a power take-off when I was a kid. There's considerable scar tissue in the calf of my leg."

Jill's eyes widened. For one terrible moment Daniel thought she was going to cry and he would do something foolish like dropping the box and pulling her into his arms to comfort her.

"Sometimes I'm such a blunderer," she said.

"Come on," Daniel said soothingly, "you couldn't know what happened. You're too softhearted. Now where shall I put these books?"

"In the walk-in closet off the master bedroom," she said. "I'm going to use the shelves for my books."

"Why not the shelves in the front room?" he asked.

"And ruin the decor?" she teased, then added seriously, "I like to read in bed. The books will be closer if I put them in the closet."

"Makes sense to me," Daniel said. He headed for the bedroom. She left the house. She was coming back down the sidewalk as he was going up. The sun caused golden highlights in her hair and the desert air carried the light scent of her perfume, lilac blossoms.

As they passed, he said, "I gather you read a lot."

"Either that or I collect books instead of knick-knacks," she said.

"You read a lot," Daniel said.

She laughed. "I might as well admit it," she said. "This load is only a part of the books I own."

They met again. This time while he was going down and she was coming up. They paused. "You said this is only a part of the books. How many loads do you have to move?"

"Two more should do it," she said.

They passed once more before the car was unloaded. Jill was coming down the incline when he was going up. She deposited her box in the closet, then went into the living room. She stood looking out the window while she waited for Daniel. What a view, she thought. The Superstition Mountains. The desert landscape. She could handle this....

"I'll go with you to help move the books," he said.

Jill hadn't heard him come into the front room. She turned to face him. "I appreciate the offer, but it isn't necessary."

"I know it isn't," he said. "But if Mother had any idea how many books you were moving, she would have volunteered both Autry and me."

Jill wondered whether he would have offered if he hadn't felt his mother would have wanted it. But she was not averse to spending some time with him. "What about your experiment?"

"I'll get to it," he said. "Do you want me to drive my car?"

"Why would I want that?" she asked as they left the apartment.

"It appears to me," he said, smiling, "that the fewer miles you put on your car, the better."

"Oh, hurt my heart, would you," Jill said. She groaned playfully, slapping the car trunk as she passed. "This old buggy might be ten years old, but since the overhaul—talk about spunk."

He met her gaze over the roof of the car. "Real get-up-and-go. Right?"

"Right."

"I'm a nonbeliever," he said.

They were chuckling as they fastened their seat belts. "Ready?" Jill asked. When he nodded, she started the car and launched into the lyrics of a popular song.

"What?" Daniel laughed.

"I always sing to Chester."

"I'm not Chester."

"So I'll sing to myself," Jill countered. She sang a few more bars before breaking off to say, "Daniel. You aren't singing. Come on. Be a sport. Sing."

"If I *must* sing, how about making it something I know?"

"Okay—go ahead," Jill agreed.

"Nobody knows the trouble I've seen," he sang in a mellow baritone.

The melancholy wasn't in the smile he was smiling in her direction, Jill decided. No. It came from deep in his eyes, down where the soul resided.

She had seen him pale at the memory of his accident. Wanting to ease the visible pain was not a personal thing, she assured herself. It was simply what she did best—help people.

"Nobody knows," Jill sang.

After the song, he slipped into thoughtfulness. She wasn't uncomfortable. She knew that when he had something to say, he would say it.

"I'm wondering why you took the administrator's position at the center," he said. "I can't help but think you liked being a social worker."

When Jill saw that she wasn't going to make the yellow at the intersection ahead, she eased to a stop. "I loved it. But my caseload kept getting heavier. There were so many problems and so few answers . . . too little time. I felt myself burning out. So I jumped at the administrator's position when I heard about it."

"The seniors must have personal problems," Daniel suggested. "Especially in the area of health."

The light changed. They came abreast of two teenagers riding bikes. She didn't take her eyes from them until she'd safely passed them.

"Of course they have problems," she agreed. "They worry about being underinsured. Overinsured. We have numerous couples where the healthy mate is providing the basic health care for the ill one . . . that's where the volunteers are such a help. Spending a few hours with the housebound mate, driving the Care car."

"So you left one set of problems for another," Daniel stated.

"There's a difference. The seniors have a positive attitude about life. They're a joy to be with," Jill said enthusiastically. "I hope when I reach senior-citizens status I'm as energetic as they are."

Daniel smiled. Forty years from now, he was sure, she'd still be filled with energy and surrounded by family and friends. Forty years from now—if he lived that long—he would be an old duffer relying on a cane while he pushed peanuts to park pigeons.

"I think when you hit eighty you'll still be running on high octane," he said.

"Is that a compliment?" Jill asked. She swerved to avoid back-ending a driver who had indicated a right turn and taken a left at the last moment.

They were approaching Superstition Freeway. Daniel braced his hand on the dash. "It was, but the way you drive—"

"Chill out, Daniel." Jill laughed. "Chester doesn't complain about my driving."

They zipped onto the freeway. "How fast are we going?" Daniel asked.

"We're *flowing* with the traffic," Jill said. "Chester doesn't worry about riding with me."

"He's a pig. What does a pig know about driving?"

"Plenty," Jill said.

For the next ten minutes they debated the intelligence of pigs. Jill took the position that pigs were very smart animals. He, tongue in cheek, she knew, argued the opposite.

When he said he'd once had a horse that could open gates, Jill asked, "Without training, how many horses will stand on their back legs and beg for peanuts? How many horses will dance unless someone snaps a whip at them? How many, Daniel?"

"All right." Daniel laughed. "Chester is a smart pig."

As she swung the car from the freeway, he reflected that Jill was unpretentious. She was natural, with a sense of fun that didn't quit. But it wasn't as if she were stuck in perpetual childhood, doing childish things. Quite the opposite. She had poise and maturity.

Eventually she whipped the car left, and turned into the driveway of her house and parked. "This is it," she said. "And the woman peeking from behind the curtain is my landlady, Mrs. Chatham."

"Is she into surveillance?" Daniel asked as he stepped from the car.

"Surveillance is a good word. Nosy is more accurate," she said. She joined him at the front of the car where she quickly explained about the women and their children, Mr. Moore and the parrot.

Daniel was laughing by the time she finished. "The parrot cursed anyone who knocked at the door?" he asked.

"The postman. The minister when he visited. And Mrs. Chatham when she made her daily sortie through the house to make sure I hadn't sneaked someone in when she wasn't looking."

Daniel chuckled.

"I'm glad you think it's funny. Mrs. Chatham didn't. She thought the parrot was being personal." Jill glanced toward the window. "See how far she's drawn back the curtain. That's because we're almost beyond her line of vision and she's wondering what we're doing."

"What we're doing is none of her business," Daniel stated.

"What gets me is that I've never given her a problem, but I'm to the point where I'd like to do something to drive her wild," Jill said. She narrowed her eyes, trying to give him a villainous expression. "I'm thinking about gluing the kitchen-cupboard doors closed before I leave."

"Tenderhearted you . . . with a mean streak?"

She snickered menacingly. "Now you know."

"I'm going to have to warn Mother how you feel about nosy landladies."

Laughing, they moved to the door. She drew her key from her purse. When they were in the house, she whistled. Chester came trotting from a bedroom.

The pig stopped in front of Daniel and rose on his back feet, begging. Daniel leaned down, scratching Chester behind the ears. "Sorry, buddy. I don't have a cookie."

Jill reached into her purse, brought out a small package of salted peanuts and handed it to Daniel. "Chester's treat."

Daniel opened the package and dumped the peanuts into the palm of his hand. Before he could offer the peanuts to Chester, she warned, "Watch him or he'll try to take the whole bunch into his mouth at once. He has a tendency to make a pig of himself."

"He is a pig."

Jill raised a finger to her lips and whispered, "Shh. He doesn't know."

Daniel smiled. He was at ease with Jill. He likened being with her to being with his family or close friends like Phoebe, Ralph and Nell. They made him laugh, also, but not like he'd laughed today. His ribs ached from it and the sensation he felt was rejuvenating.

He hunkered down eyeball-to-eyeball with Chester and slipped the pig a peanut. "How old are you?" he asked.

"Eight months."

Daniel pivoted on his heel, looked up at her. "Not Chester. *You.* How old are you?"

"By day count, thirty-three," Jill said. "By any other measure, I'm as old as I want to be."

"So, you'll always be younger than springtime," he said, his voice softly weighted with emotions he didn't understand.

She rescued him from embarrassment by saying, "That was beautifully expressed, Daniel. Thank you. And how old are you?"

"By day count, forty."

"I was guessing thirty-five. And how old are you by any other count?"

Daniel slipped the last peanut to Chester, rubbed the pig behind the ears, then stood. "By any count, I'm forty."

"So old!" Jill teased. "The books are in the spare bedroom, but now I'm wondering if you'll last the day if you help carry them."

She amazed him, Daniel reflected. Thirty-three— she appeared younger. Her making a jest of his being forty made him wonder why he worried about it. Because he did worry when he allowed himself to think about how old he was, how much he had left to do. He thought about how he had already lived more of his life than he had to live.

Jill's smile lifted the burden of his thoughts. "I may be forty, but I'm not out of condition," he retorted. "Lead the way to the books."

Twenty minutes later, while Jill locked the house, Daniel was shoving the last box of books into the back seat when he felt something brush his leg, and heard a grunt.

Thinking Jill had locked the house but forgotten about Chester, he called, "Chester's with me."

"I promised him he could go along this trip," she called back.

"Where is he going to ride? In your lap so he can drive?"

She jogged to the car. "Oh, no. Chester always rides on the passenger seat. He's the copilot."

"I'm on the passenger seat," Daniel reminded her.

"That's true." She laughed. "But I didn't know you'd be along when I promised Chester a ride on the next trip I made. He won't mind riding on your lap."

Daniel had visions of Jill hitting seventy, weaving in and out of traffic on Superstition Freeway, as he held Chester, the copilot.

"Well, hell," he said. "Let's go."

They did draw attention. Even at seventy, people passed them and then craned their necks, looking back. Daniel could see lips moving, saying, "Yes. That man is holding a pig in his lap."

They were driving down Main Street in Mesa when Jill asked, "Mind if we stop for an ice-cream cone?"

It appeared to Daniel that she had already made the decision because she was changing lanes to get to a parlor advertising one hundred flavors. But he didn't mind.

"Okay," he said.

Before they had parked, Chester began squirming in Daniel's arms. Jill glanced at him.

"I know, Chester," she said. "You want your usual. Want to sit at an umbrella table to eat?"

Chester grunted again.

"Not you, Chester," she said. "I was asking Daniel."

"You were asking me?"

"Of course. Chester always wants to have his cone at the umbrella table."

"He does, does he?"

"He does."

"I don't believe one word of it," Daniel said as they piled out of the car. "But I am wondering whether or not I should set him down to walk."

"Of course," Jill said. "He won't stray. And you should believe me because you'll soon have proof of it."

Daniel set Chester to the ground. Chester trotted ahead, his hooves clicking merrily on the cement. Daniel was not totally surprised when the girl at the outside service window greeted Jill like an old friend.

"Hello, Jill." She leaned forward, over the counter. "How are you doing, Chester? Want your usual?"

Chester arched his neck to look up. The neck hide rolled in puckers. He grunted twice. "Got it. Chocolate. Medium," the girl said. "Strawberry chocolate swirl for you, Jill," she stated. "And you, sir?"

"Vanilla," Daniel said.

Jill murmured, "One hundred flavors and you want vanilla?"

"Call me pedestrian."

"You're anything but prosaic."

Daniel might have responded but a family of three joined the line and he was distracted by a little dark-haired girl.

"Is that a real pig, mister?" the little girl asked.
Daniel smiled. "He's real."

"Can I touch his nose?" the little girl asked, as her mother tried to shush her.

"Well..." Daniel looked at Jill. "Sure. Go ahead."

The little girl dropped to her knees, extended a tentative finger to Chester's nose. He responded by sniffing. The little girl giggled and Jill's laughter acted like a festive invitation to everyone in the vicinity.

In a few short minutes Chester and Jill had captured and enchanted a small audience. Jill was pelted with questions about Chester. She patiently explained about potbellied pigs and the great pets they made.

The cones arrived. Jill slipped her hand into her purse, but Daniel stopped her, saying, "My treat."

A few minutes later they were seated at the table. As Jill licked her cone, she held Chester's at knee level. Chester nipped off the cone's peak, then ate downward.

Again, a group of children materialized from nowhere to gather around them. Jill seemed to give each child her full attention as she talked with them about Chester. They showed no fear, no reserve in talking to her. Several even draped an arm over her shoulder while they visited. She returned the favor with a hug around their waists.

Strange, Daniel thought, the feeling he was feeling. He had lived his life being driven by the feeling that there were only so many ticks of the clock and not one tick should be wasted. And yet here he was, sharing the afternoon with a potbellied pig and a gregarious, lovely young woman and he wasn't restless, nagged by the feeling he should be doing something else.

But it would end quickly enough. They would unload the books, make one last trip and then the interlude would be over. Jill would involve herself in the lives of other people and he would slip back into his private world. No harm done.

Chapter Five

"What are you thinking?" she asked.

Daniel came from thought to realize that for the moment they were alone. "I was thinking how you seem to draw children to you," he said.

"I do love children," she said. "Wish I had a dozen of them. Or two." She laughed. "Yes. Two probably would be all I could handle. But it's Chester who draws the children. They love him."

"No. It's you," Daniel stated. "Children *and* adults are drawn to you because they know you enjoy being with them."

"And you don't?" Jill asked. "Or is it that you prefer your own company?"

She was reading between the lines and drawing erroneous conclusions. He did like people. Preferring to be by himself had been a learned thing.

He smiled lazily. "It would be a waste of time to try to figure me out," he said.

Jill blotted her lips with a paper napkin. He didn't know it, but he had just issued her a challenge that she couldn't refuse. Eventually, she figured everybody out. "Ready to go?" she asked.

"Ready," he said.

Less than two hours later they were back at Jill's place, ready to pick up the last load of books. She had felt guilty about taking Daniel away from his work, but he had insisted. And she hadn't resisted.

She knew he was not trying to manipulate her. Therefore he was *safe*. Beyond that, she liked him. They had talked almost nonstop about everything from football to the desert landscape.

When she parked the car, she automatically glanced to Mrs. Chatham's house. "She's still at it," she stated.

She slipped from the car. Daniel opened the car door, set Chester to the ground. "Have you told her that you'll be moving?" he asked as she shut the door.

"In a manner of speaking," Jill said, recalling how she'd called out to Mrs. Chatham earlier. "I'll send her a registered letter tomorrow. Meanwhile, I'm sure she's concluded that I've found another place. There's no doubt in my mind what's really bugging her is wondering who you are."

They ambled toward the door, Chester trotting ahead of them. "And what are you going to tell her?" Daniel asked.

"What am I going to tell her?" she asked rhetorically. She unlocked the door, shoved it open, grinned over her shoulder, back at Daniel. "I'll tell her that you're my sweetheart. Wondering where I found you will drive her crazy."

Laughing, Daniel closed the door, followed her into the front room and headed for the bedroom. Jill delayed him by laying her hand on his arm.

"Before we get the books," she said, "close your eyes."

"Close my eyes?"

"Just do it and then I'll explain what I have in mind."

"You're planning to seduce me?"

Jill was in the process of tossing her purse to the sofa. She missed. The purse fell to the floor with a plunk. She glanced at him, saw the glimmer of merriment in his eyes. Chuckling, she bent to retrieve her purse.

"That was a shocker," she said.

"I don't know why it would be," Daniel said. "You're the one who said I was your sweetheart."

Jill smiled; she couldn't help it. Daniel was at least ninety percent warm and spontaneous. The other ten percent—defense? Or guarding against being hurt?

"Rest easy, Daniel Holiday," she said. She balled her fist and rapped him lightly on the shoulder. "Women don't seduce men."

"I know women who try."

Jill considered that a moment. He was probably speaking from experience. And he hadn't liked it. "I know there are," she agreed. "I was speaking personally." She laughed. "Now, please. Close your eyes. I promise not to breathe hot breaths past your ear."

He slipped his fingers into his jean pockets, propped a shoulder against the wall. "To breathe past my ear, you'd have to stand on a chair."

"You're procrastinating," Jill said. "Close them." When he did, she said, "I want to see how good you really are at recall—"

"Is this normal entertainment for you?" he asked. "Having men close their eyes so you can test them for recall?"

"No, Daniel. This is not normal entertainment for me. You're special—" His lashes fluttered. "—No peeking! What's in this room?"

"You are strange."

Jill smiled. He had made *strange* sound beautiful, charming, intelligent. Wonderful. "Can't do it?" she asked.

He listed twenty-five or thirty items in quick succession. "Pretty good?" he asked as he opened his eyes.

"Pretty good? The only thing you missed was yesterday's newspaper."

"I did?" He straightened, made a quick survey of the room. "Where is it?"

"Under the sofa," Jill said. She snickered. He pulled his hands free of his jeans, made a playful gesture of wringing her neck. "All kidding aside," she said, "with recall like that, you must have cruised through school."

"I did," Daniel said. "But it didn't make me especially popular. Well, we'd better get moving."

He headed toward the bedroom, leaving Jill to trail. His friendly attitude had not changed, but he was definitely subdued. Being smart hadn't made him especially popular?

She had been a good student. But she had never felt her intelligence made her unpopular. However, she wasn't a genius, which she suspected Daniel might be, even though aside from his theory about developing high, rapid heat on low amounts of energy there'd been nothing in their conversation that would give him away. He didn't talk down to her, but treated her as an equal.

They worked in silence as they loaded the car. But their frequent exchange of smiles spoke eloquently, Jill decided. It was Daniel, while standing in the middle of the front room holding the last box of books, who broke the silence.

"You must have disliked living here," he said.

Jill had slipped her purse to her shoulder, extended her hand to open the door for him. She turned as he turned toward her. "What makes you think that?" she asked.

"You have a penchant for color. The bedspread and curtains are you," Daniel said. "As are the pillows and rugs you've used to brighten rooms. But the neutral colors in the sofa and chair, on the walls. That isn't you."

"You're right," Jill admitted. "But I didn't dislike the house. I simply felt no personal attachment to it. In regard to my liking bright colors," she added, smiling, "I have a friend who designs clothes. Abbey says I'm the only one she knows who would dare wear a purple polka-dot blouse with red plaid shorts."

"I don't know about the polka-dot-plaid combination, but I do know that not many women could wear red and yellow flowers blossoming all over them and look as good as you do," Daniel said. "I like your outfit. Very much."

Jill hadn't thought he'd noticed what she was wearing. That he had pleased her inordinately. She opened the door and held it open while he passed through.

"Thank you," she said.

After making sure Chester was following Daniel, Jill locked the door and slipped the key in her purse. By the time she reached the car, Daniel had loaded the box into the back seat and was standing, looking to where Mrs. Chatham was framed in her window.

"Good grief," he muttered. "I've never seen such a blatant display of nosiness."

Jill waved at Mrs. Chatham. "It's a good thing I'm moving, because she really is getting on my nerves."

"Understandable," Daniel said. "Go ahead and do it."

"Do it?"

"Glue shut the cupboard doors before you leave."

"Don't encourage me—I know!" Jill exploded with glee. "Kiss me!"

"Kiss you?"

"Just on the cheek," Jill said. "It won't take much to drive Mrs. Chatham's inquisitiveness off the Richter scale. But if I'm asking too much, say so."

She was not asking too much, Daniel thought. Any man would like to kiss her. He'd like to kiss her. And he couldn't deny that the thought hadn't been with him all day. He wouldn't mind holding her, either. . . .

He extended his arms. She slid into them. He embraced her gingerly. She started to chuckle. "Daniel. If you're going to embrace me, it won't fool Mrs. Chatham if you hold me like a crisp cracker."

There were green diamonds of laughter in her eyes. Daniel laughed with her, but he was already thinking he had made a mistake. She was capable of playing this kind of game effortlessly and coming away from it laughing. Now that he had tempted himself by holding her, he wasn't sure that he could.

Barely touching Jill was titilating. Drawing her closer would be torment. But he drew her closer, then closer still, until the most observant viewer would be deceived into thinking the gesture was intimate. And the feel of her *was* exquisite. Beneath the daintiness, she was lush, deliciously woman, a perfect blend of roundness of breast, smallness of waist and bigness of heart.

"You see," she said. She smiled up at him, her head slightly tilted, the long mane of golden hair wisping over his fingers. "I don't break."

Daniel's heart pounded, pulsed like a hammer in his head. Holding her seemed natural. But he cautioned himself to manage the situation with the same kind of cool detachment one would use in directing a play.

Move your hand to her chin. When he did, her smile softened. *Caress her face. Trace the peach roundness of her cheeks.* When he did, the expression in her eyes turned puzzled.

Daniel wasn't aware that the nature of the game had changed, Jill thought dully. But she knew. In the last light of day, before Mrs. Chatham, before Chester and all of the neighbors, she was being seduced.

She hadn't expected more than a fleeting kiss. Now as his thumb wandered from her cheek to lightly trace the outline of her lips, she wanted more than a brushing encounter.

The fingers of his free hand stroked through her hair. He cupped her head, bent and kissed her. Tentatively. Teasingly. Jill kissed him back unreservedly.

Suddenly Daniel realized that emotions, not pragmatic thought, had taken over. He abruptly lifted his lips, looked over Jill's head to Mrs. Chatham's window. The woman's mouth was agape. In shock, he supposed.

Jill found herself standing alone, trying to sort through a residue of emotions. When she raised her eyes to Daniel's face, she saw that he was looking past her to Mrs. Chatham's window.

"I think that was demonstration enough to fool Mrs. Chatham," he said.

Jill glanced over her shoulder. Mrs. Chatham had one hand on her chest, the other fanning her face. Then the curtain fell.

In her glance to the window, Jill had hoped to compose herself. What she'd felt wasn't related to *helping* him. What she'd felt was his closeness alive in ways she had never imagined. And she was ill prepared to deal with it because it was so unexpected.

Jill forced her gaze back to Daniel. "It was some demonstration," she said. "Very convincing."

She witnessed something dark and hurtful swirling in Daniel's eyes. Then, like a mist settling over the mountains, he obliterated the emotion. The chill coming from him was tangible.

"Don't be fooled," he said tersely. "You interest me. But no woman holds my interest long." He glanced at his watch. "It's late."

Without looking at her he walked around the car, opened the door, bent and picked up Chester. He settled into the car before glancing at Jill.

"I'm coming," Jill murmured. Was she deceiving herself again as she had with Stephen? Was Daniel really arrogant, not lonely? Did his ego need stroking or was it already inflated?

No. She hadn't miscalculated. No man could kiss a woman as tenderly as he had kissed her and be uncaring. The callous verbal attack was the facade. But his sharpness still hurt.

She opened the door and slid into the car. She fastened her seat belt. He settled Chester on his lap and fastened his seat belt. He finally looked at her.

"We're ready," he said.

"I'm not starting the car until I've had my say," she said, sounding wintry. "I am not attempting to invade your privacy."

Daniel couldn't pretend that he didn't know she was hurt and angry. She was straightforward in allowing him to see it. But how did he tell this free-spirited, endearing woman that she frightened him? That it was desperation that caused him to utter mean, belittling words.

Something was wrong with his logic and he knew it. Jill Fulbright would not deride him, try to belittle him. She would stand her ground with him and rightly so.

Lacking the ability to explain himself, he said, "I'm sorry if I hurt your feelings."

"That's a beginning," Jill said. Her fingers drummed on the steering wheel. "But why did you say what you did, Daniel?"

He looked away, straight ahead. "Because I'm a cad. Start the car."

"Not yet. You're no cad."

"A jerk, then. Let's go. Chester's squirming."

"Let him squirm—you're no jerk, either."

"All right," he said. "It's been my experience that women need more attention than I can give them. Okay?"

Jill started the car, backed slowly from the driveway. "I don't know that I'm prepared to accept your apology," she said. "I don't like being lumped with women in general."

"I am truly and deeply sorry," Daniel said. "And from this moment, I'll try to remember to respect your feelings and not lump you with women in general."

"I hear the sound of laughter in your voice, Daniel. Are you laughing at me or with me?"

The wintry tone was gone from her voice, Daniel reflected. His name coming from her lips now sounded like the warmth of a spring breeze. "With you," he said. "Am I forgiven?"

"I'm thinking about it," she said. She chuckled softly. "Okay. You're forgiven."

They crossed the city, unloaded the books. Daniel was carrying the last box to the closet when he admitted to himself that he was thankful that once Jill had forgiven him, she had dropped the subject. He hadn't known what else to tell her, and it was much better this way... back on easy street with each other. Talking freely. Teasing. No subterfuge.

After placing the box on the floor of the closet, he went into the front room and found Jill standing in front of the window, gazing into the valley.

"What are you thinking?" he asked as he joined her.

Jill laughed. "What makes you think I was thinking anything?"

"I would venture you are never without a thought," he said.

"I was thinking I'm going to enjoy this view and thinking how when I first arrived in the valley from Iowa, I didn't think I was going to survive the heat and barrenness. I was thinking how I learned that the desert blossoms and reveals all kinds of secrets. I was thinking how the desert has grown on me." She smiled and winked. "Sorry you asked?"

His gaze drifted from hers into the valley, then to the Superstition Mountains. "We've been here ten years and I'm still gaining an appreciation for the desert," he stated. "Ever think of giving some away?"

She frowned. "Some of what?"

"Books," he said. "I see you read everything from fiction to history."

"I couldn't," Jill said. "Once I read a book, even if it's bad, I can't get rid of it."

"I'm the same way. I have books in my library I know I will never read again, but I can't get rid of them," he said. "Feel free to use my library while you're here."

She nodded and smiled. My God, Daniel thought. Her gaze was drawing him in, triggering coded messages that tracked up his spine, made him question ideas he had long ago thought he had resolved logically. Questions about falling in love and destiny.

Love, he believed, was something other people fell into but he couldn't. And destiny was the excuse people used when they tried to explain how they'd happened to fall in love with the wrong person.

"There was one more thing I was thinking about— wondering about, actually," she said.

"Something to do with the house? The garage, maybe," he suggested. "There's an extra stall. You can use it."

She laughed. "Nothing like that. I was thinking that you seem to be as cautious about relationships as Autry seems impulsive. That's all."

All! Daniel thought. In a nutshell? "Autry isn't quite as impulsive as you might think," he said. "But I suppose cautious does apply to me, even though I tend to trust my first impressions of a person."

She nodded. "Me, too. In the past, when I ignored that inner voice, I discovered myself in a heap of trouble."

"A man?"

"A man."

"And your first impression of him was?"

"That he was totally self-centered and wallowing in self-pity," she responded without hesitation.

Daniel settled on the arm of an overstuffed chair. "He was wallowing in self-pity because he'd been hurt. You felt sorry for him and before you knew it, you were involved with him. Right?"

Jill studied Daniel's expression but was unsuccessful in even guessing what he was thinking. But she thought he should know that he wasn't alone in having failed at past relationships.

"Steve played on my sympathy, all right," she admitted. "He'd been married twice and divorced both times. He told me that all he wanted out of life was a faithful, loving wife and children. He was lying. What he wanted was an uncomplicated physical relationship."

"No man with a sense of self-worth would play on a woman's sympathy," he stated.

"He was a true cad," she said, smiling.

"I was thinking turkey."

Jill laughed. "That he was, but I really couldn't place all the blame on him. Some of the problem was me," she admitted. "I think I wanted to be involved. Wanted to fall in love. Do you know what I mean?"

He rocked back on the arm of the chair as if physically doodling while he considered his answer. He came forward. Chester was lying at his feet. He reached down and rubbed the pig between the ears.

After what Jill thought was an aeon, he looked up at her. "Yes," he said. "I do know what you mean."

Jill glanced back into the valley. The lights of the city were on. It was time to go. "I've resolved not to misread my motivations again," she said. She half laughed. "And to forevermore trust my first impression."

She turned from the window and walked in the direction of the door. He followed. Chester trotted after him. They were outside, walking up the incline, when Jill added, "If you're curious, I'm positive my first impressions of you aren't going to change one iota once I get to know you."

He laughed. "That I'm brusque and self-centered?"

They had reached the car. Jill leaned against the door. Daniel stood with his elbow propped on the roof. "I think you aren't as aloof as you pretend to be. That the memory of your accident caused you pain."

With his free hand Daniel reached to brush a strand of hair back over her ear. Too late he realized the intimacy of the gesture but was saved from embarrassment because he realized she had not read intimacy into it. When he dropped his hand she simply reached up and completed pushing her hair back into place.

He answered carefully. "I'll admit that memory is not among my favorites." He tried a smile.

"My goodness," she said. "Now you're getting mysterious."

Daniel realized that she was trying to give him an opening to talk. But he had to remember that she was doing it because that was what she was trained to do, what her nature demanded her to do. He was not special. And he certainly didn't want to play on her sympathy as Steve had.

"I don't think I'm mysterious," he said.

"Secretive, then."

Daniel straightened. "When you get to know me," he said, "you'll discover that I'm neither mysterious nor secretive. I'm only eccentric. Have a safe drive home."

Jill scooped Chester up as Daniel opened the door. She leaned into the car and settled Chester on the passenger seat. "Copilot in place," she said, then climbed into the car. "Good night, Daniel. Thank you for the help."

"Good night, Jill."

Daniel left for his workshop before Jill started the car. "Confession time, Chester," she said as he disappeared inside and a light came on. "I like him. But he doesn't want me to get close to him."

But did she want to break through to him? What about how she'd felt when his fingers brushed her cheek? Her breath had caught and she hadn't wanted to breathe again. She'd only wanted to luxuriate in the pampering sensation.

And then . . . there was the kiss . . .

So was she prepared to get close to Daniel? Was she as calm and detached as she believed? Or would she be wise to remember the mistakes she'd made with Steve?

Chapter Six

The following morning Jill hadn't had time to make coffee when Nell bustled into her office, her expression troubled.

"Matthew Duncan had a stroke Saturday night," she said.

Jill moved from the credenza, slipped her arm around Nell's waist and guided her to a chair, then sat herself. Hattie and Matthew were one of the younger couples who attended the center on a fairly regular basis.

Nell's corkscrew curls jumped as she shook her head. "Sixty-two. Just retired," she said. "Isn't it awful?"

"Do you know how bad it is?" Jill asked.

Nell sighed. "You know Hattie. She gets a hangnail and she thinks she's dying. But Matthew's in the hospital and a stroke is bad no matter what."

The Duncans' children lived in Canada and ran the family furniture business. Hattie didn't drive. Jill asked Nell where Matthew had been admitted and jotted down the hospital name on her notepad.

"I'll try to contact Hattie later," Jill said. "If she needs transportation to and from the hospital, I'll arrange for the Care car to take her."

"Her granddaughter is already here," Nell said. "The one who's a show girl in Las Vegas. But Hattie's going to need help. That's for sure. She's one of the old school, you understand. She never worked outside her home. Matthew took care of everything. I doubt that Hattie even knows what kind of insurance they have."

"You know we'll do everything we can do to help Hattie now and after Matthew gets out of the hospital," Jill said.

"I know you will," Nell said. She went on to talk about her husband, Herman, and the stroke he had suffered. While Jill made soft, comforting sounds, Nell told of the weeks and months of doctor's appointments and physical therapy.

When Nell paused, Jill suggested, "When we see exactly what the Duncans are up against, we'll be in a better position to know how Hattie is going to handle it."

"Right," Nell agreed. "But the granddaughter told me she can only stay two weeks. A daughter is flying down now. And a son." She shook her head again. "But eventually, Hattie will be alone."

"She won't be alone. She'll have all of the regulars at the center to act as a support group," Jill said as Shauna breezed into the office.

After Shauna said hello, Nell told her about Matthew Duncan. Shauna propped herself on the edge of the desk. "My goodness," she said sadly. "Matthew? He seemed so healthy. He intended to sign up for the citywide senior tennis tournament starting next month."

"He's been playing regularly with Ralph, Phoebe and Belle," Nell said. "Ralph thought—with Matthew being so young and all—that he had a good shot at winning the singles." She sighed heavily. "But we never know, do we?"

"You aren't getting down, are you, Nell?" Jill asked.

Nell half laughed. "I was thinking about it." She smiled, first at Jill, then at Shauna. "But with you two at the helm of this ship of old duffers, I know you wouldn't allow me to feel sorry for myself even if I wanted to."

Shauna laughed. "You're wonderful, Nell."

Nell hoisted herself from the chair. "That's a fact," she said. "By the way, Jill. Did Autry ask you out?"

"Nell! Really. What a question."

"Well—did he?"

"No, he did not."

"Darn," Nell muttered. "I bet Ralph fifty cents that Autry would. Wait until I talk to that boy."

Shauna grinned at Jill and followed Nell from the office. Jill went to make the coffee.

Later, she called the hospital and talked with Hattie. She learned Matthew had suffered a light stroke and that the extent of the damage wasn't known. Jill reminded Hattie about the Care car. Hattie thanked her, commenting that she had always wanted to learn to drive but that Matthew had been against it. Now she wished she had.

After visiting with Hattie, she thought about what the woman had said about wishing she'd learned to drive. Besides Hattie, Jill knew there were at least four seniors who were fully capable of learning to drive but were dependent on the Care car, a taxi service or the goodwill of friends to do such things as get weekly groceries or get to the doctor's office.

On impulse she contacted the center for adult education to inquire about the feasibility of holding a driver's education course at the senior citizens' center. She learned it was a definite possibility, providing enough seniors wanted to learn to drive, or would take the course to brush up on their driving skills.

By the end of the day Jill felt she'd accomplished a tremendous amount. As usual, the feeling of achievement resulted in a boost of energy. She looked forward to a quick trip to the Holiday house to unload the boxes she'd packed into the car that morning. Then she would head home to Chester and more packing. After that, she would treat herself to a long bath.

Monday's trip was the first of five trips Jill would make through the week to the Holiday house. And the pattern set on Monday would remain basically the same throughout the week.

Autry never failed to pop up the moment she arrived. He helped carry boxes to the apartment. They bantered while he did. She had liked Autry when she first met him, and nothing happened to change her mind. But there certainly was no mystery about him.

Nell never failed to pop into Jill's office the moment she arrived at the center. Phoebe was often with her. By Friday morning, Nell had lost two and a half dollars to Ralph, betting when Autry was going to ask Jill out.

Nell was rather testy about Autry's failure to live up to her expectations. She was no less testy in telling Jill she was dragging her feet when it came to Autry.

Knowing Daniel was away, Jill had not expected to see him. But not seeing him hadn't kept her from thinking about him. This was especially true at the end of the day, after her bath. She would be propped up in bed, trying to read one of the science texts she had checked out at the library.

Then her mind would drift. *The kiss. The touch.* The more effort she put into trying to forget, the more vividly she remembered. She was finally forced to admit that she had never fully explored the sensual side of her nature. She had always been . . . in check. Was she hopelessly old-fashioned? Or had she never met the man who would test her?

On Saturday morning when Nell came into the office and sat down, Jill knew they were in for a longer conversation than usual.

After telling Jill that there was a good possibility that Matthew would be getting out of the hospital on Monday, but would be going to physical therapy for a couple of months, Nell asked, "Did you see Autry last night?"

"Yes."

"And what happened?"

"He helped carry boxes from the car to the apartment."

"That's it?"

"That's it," Jill said. "I suppose you lost another fifty cents to Ralph?"

Nell pouted briefly, then brightened perceptibly. "Did you know Autry's taking Hattie's granddaughter out tonight? The show girl—"

"I know. From Las Vegas," Jill said. She laughed. "How did you manage that?"

"How do you think?" Nell asked. "I called Autry and told him about Hattie's granddaughter—how she was free tonight if he was interested."

"Tell you what, Nell," Jill said slowly. "If the show girl doesn't work out, why don't you try to fix Autry up with Shauna? I think Autry and Shauna would—"

She found herself talking to Nell's back. Nell called as she stepped from the office, "Phoebe. Do I have a great idea!"

Jill smiled. Mission accomplished. The matchmakers were Shauna's problem now. But fixing Autry up with Shauna wasn't a bad idea. In fact, they were perfect for each other, both bright and filled with energy. Absolutely perfect.

That evening Jill was a little later than usual arriving at the Holiday house. As she parked, she glanced toward the workshop. There was a light on. Daniel was back.

Of course she wouldn't go to the door and knock. That would be an invasion of his privacy, and she respected his right to privacy. But she sent a mental message. *Daniel. Step out. Say hello.*

The door to the building did open, but it was Autry who stepped out. He waved and called, "Just saying hello to big brother."

Jill slipped from the car and closed the door. From Autry's calling to her, Daniel had to know she had arrived. The least he could have done was to have stepped out the door and waved. The very least.

"I don't have much," Jill said as Autry approached. She unlocked the trunk. "A few more clothes. A few dresses. A box of pots and pans that I know I won't be using this week. I really don't need help."

"No problem," Autry said. "Between the two of us we ought to make short work of it." He grabbed a box from the trunk.

They did make short work of the unloading. Last in were dresses Jill seldom wore. They were on hangers in plastic protectors.

After the clothes were hung, Autry appraised the rod space left in the closet. "You need more clothes," he stated.

"Or less closet," Jill said.

"More clothes," Autry asserted. "Top-of-the-line kind of stuff."

Jill had seen him assessing her clothes. "Fess up, Autry. When you say top of the line, what you really mean is that you have misgivings about the clothes I own."

"Misgivings is a little strong," Autry countered. He followed Jill from the closet, across the bedroom and back to the kitchen to where they'd left the box of pans. "It's just that I can see you in lush green, black. Something simple."

"Slinky, maybe?"

"Now you're talking."

Jill smiled. Daniel did like her choice in clothes, even though he hadn't come from his hideaway to say hello. "I do have one green dress," she said.

"Sexy?"

Jill squelched further comment with a frown, crouched down and opened the cupboard door next to the stove to put the pans away. The space was filled to capacity. "I hope there's an empty cupboard."

She started her search, locating an empty cupboard under the breakfast bar.

"What makes me think I'm not making the kind of impression on you that I'd like?" Autry asked. "Could it be because while I'm talking about sexy clothes you're more interested in where you're going to put a bunch of pots and pans?"

Jill looked up to where Autry was leaning over the breakfast bar looking down, a smile on his face. He was truly likable and she did have fun bantering with him but that was the extent of it—and always would be the extent of it.

"Aren't you going to be late for your date?" she asked. She quickly stored the pots and pans.

"How did you know I had a date?"

"Nell happened to mention it five or six times today. And she was only at the center an hour," Jill said. She stood and set the cardboard box on the counter between them. "Hattie's granddaughter. The show girl. From Las Vegas."

Autry rolled his shoulders in a shucks gesture. "I told Nell you wouldn't flick an eyelash but she had this idea that my taking out a show girl would make you jealous."

"We're going to be good friends," Jill said.

"I get the impression there are no sparks on your part. Right?"

"Right," she admitted.

"Story of my life," Autry said. "Every woman I would truly be interested in getting to know better is involved with someone else." He grabbed the empty box from the counter because Jill was taking it back with her.

Jill picked up her purse, shut off the kitchen light and walked toward the entry. "I'm not interested in anyone else," she said.

Autry flipped off the entry light, followed Jill outside and waited while she locked the door. "So if I called in sick to my date, would you have dinner with me?"

"And how much did Nell pay you to ask?"

"Not a thing," Autry said. He chuckled. "But she bet Ralph three bucks that I'd ask tonight even if I did have a date with Hattie's granddaughter."

"What a shyster!"

"Hard not to love her, isn't it?" Autry asked.

Laughing, they walked to Jill's car. Autry tossed the box in the trunk and closed the lid. Jill nibbled her lip. She shouldn't ask. But she had to.

"I suppose Daniel is working?"

"Unless Daniel is tramping the mountains around Sedona, spending a few days in Iowa or time at his company in Chicago, he's working on his experiments," Autry said.

"He has a business in Chicago?"

"The five engineers and designers who work for him are located there. Belldan is the company name."

Jill was sure there was a bean buggy carrying that name. The seats were on a suspension system mounted on the front of a tractor and lifted up and down by a hydraulic system. Instead of a farmer hiring twenty people to walk a bean field to pull weeds, he hired four to ride the buggy. As the tractor traversed the field of soybeans, the riders squirted a dab of weed killer on the weeds.

"Isn't there a Belldan bean buggy?" she asked.

Autry laughed. "The tractor mount was Daniel's first invention."

"But he isn't old enough! That's been on the market for years," Jill said. "I made summer money when I was in high school riding for farmers in the area."

"Daniel was sixteen when he developed the mounted bean buggy. Twenty-four when he developed a one-rider, self-propelled three-wheeler," Autry said. "In the case of the bean buggies, he sold the patent to a manufacturer. But with some of his products, he's licensed a manufacturer for the actual production."

"He was sixteen when he started inventing—"

"Daniel has *always* been innovating, modifying or inventing," Autry said proudly. "He graduated from college with a degree in business before he was twenty. He was also well on the way to making his first million."

Now some of the signals Daniel had given her—the significant silences, the quick changes in topic, the statement that being smart hadn't made him popular—began to make sense.

"You say he graduated from college at twenty?"

"Right. And high school at fourteen. He stayed home for a couple of years farming full-time," Autry explained. "He put the first buggy together in the farm workshop. He was also working on a scale system that could be attached to a grinder. But he didn't patent that until five or six years ago."

Jill hadn't missed hearing the unabashed pride sounding in Autry's voice when he talked about his brother. As for herself, she was stung. By no stretch of the definition could anyone say Daniel had had a *normal* teenage passage.

"I hadn't realized," Jill said. Her gaze fastened on Daniel's building. But how stupid she really had been not to have realized. Daniel had as much as drawn a picture for her. The competition for his attention was not another woman, but what was going on in his mind.

"The fact is," Autry said, "Daniel has always been my protector, my best friend. Without his financial backing when I launched the construction business, I couldn't have gotten enough money together to build a doghouse."

"I'm sure you would have been successful without him," Jill said.

"Thank you, my friend," Autry said.

"I mean it."

"I know you mean it." Autry laughed. "But you haven't taken your eyes from Daniel's workshop. So why don't you just walk over, pop in and chat a bit?"

"No," Jill said decisively. "If he's working, I don't want to interrupt and risk having him toss me out— yes. I am going to say hello."

Autry laughed. "Changing your mind in one breath. Dare I wonder aloud if that isn't just like a woman?"

Jill tossed him a playfully scathing look, then marched in the direction of Daniel's hideaway.

Daniel stared at the worktable. He told himself now that he was back, with time to concentrate, he was thinking his usual deep thoughts. He told himself that because he had flux and a flux brush and the solder out, he was ready to do a little experimenting.

He knew Jill was here.

He even went so far as to admit that he had enjoyed the day he'd spent with her. This evening, when his mother had reminded him about a pen for Chester, he'd assured her that he hadn't forgotten. When she had bombarded him with news from the center, praising Jill Fulbright for her management of a difficult problem confronting one of the couples, he had listened with interest.

"She cares about people," Belle had said.

He had nodded, but thought, *Like I don't know Jill cares about people.* He had thought about that very thing from time to time through the week, and reaffirmed to himself that she was a toucher of people. Children had allowed themselves to be embraced by her, knowing intuitively she could be trusted.

The problem was him. Could he trust himself to keep a clear understanding that Jill, because she was Jill, cared about him because she cared about *everyone* she met? He was not some *significant other....*

"Daniel?"

Daniel looked to the door. He had told himself she wouldn't come. He had wished she would come. Then he could blame her, and not himself, for his inability to concentrate.

And there she was, her golden blouse and slacks matching the color of her hair.

"You're color coordinated," he said.

"I'm color coordinated?"

He turned the impending compliment into a rudimentary comment. "Your blouse. Slacks. They match," he said. "It's the first time you haven't been wearing flowers."

She chuckled. "I take that as an affirmative that I can come into your hideaway."

Like a beam of sunlight flowing through the window, she moved from the door to his workbench. "Mother tells me you had a big week at the center," he said.

She studied the equipment he'd set out. Without looking up at him, she said, "No busier than usual. Except for Matthew Duncan's problem."

"Mother mentioned the man had a stroke," Daniel said. "I've never met the Duncans, but they have my sympathy."

His mental balance was threatened by her. He understood that. What he didn't understand was why. He was too damn old for infatuation, too damn smart not to understand chemistry. There had to be a reason she got to him. There *had* to be.

"Hattie is going to begin a driver's education course in two weeks," Jill said, looking up to meet his gaze. "That is, providing Matthew continues to improve physically. Right now he's depressed and fighting the efforts of the hospital staff to help him."

"And what are you going to do about that?" he asked, knowing she would try to do something.

"Right now, nothing," she said. She pulled up a stool and climbed on, making herself comfortable. "After he's out of the hospital, if he is still depressed, that's when we'll start working on him."

"Working on him?" Daniel asked.

She laughed. "Sounds like a bad choice of words, doesn't it? But, yes, we'll work on him. Matthew feels vulnerable for the first time in his life. For the first time in his life, he isn't making the decisions for himself and his family. He's dependent upon other people. We'll work on him, show him that he can regain a certain amount of independence—"

"Maybe a certain amount of independence won't be enough," Daniel suggested. "Not for a man who has been responsible for himself and his family."

"In my opinion," she said slowly, "it is always wrong when a man assumes a patriarchal role, or a woman a matriarchal role. When one mate assumes sole authority, the other assumes a submissive or passive role. Right?"

There was something in the way she asked the question that caused Daniel to reflect that she was asking him to question himself. About what, he didn't know. He'd never assumed a patriarchal role. He'd only assumed the responsibility of providing for his mother and Autry after his father's death.

"Having no experience in the area, you're asking a poor authority," he said. He turned to lean against the bench.

"But you must have an opinion," she insisted. "You witnessed the dynamics between your parents and your aunts and uncles."

"My aunts and uncles...a mixed bag on both sides," Daniel said. "Dad would have liked to have been a dictator, I think. At least he had a good role model. My grandfather had no tolerance for anyone who questioned his authority. Especially one of his children."

Daniel paused, not knowing quite how far he should go with this. "I'm sure you know the pattern," he said. "Question his authority, and he saw it as an act of belligerence. His standard threat was the old standby—do as I say or I'll disown you." Daniel laughed. "That bull worked on my aunt, but not with my dad because my mother held her own with both my grandfather and my dad. Especially when it came to me.... Autry, too, of course."

"Hattie never learned to hold her own with Matthew," Jill said. "And now she wishes she had.... I know you're working." She smiled. "And I don't want to keep you from it, but I've been wondering...is it possible to use a vacuum tube?"

"A vacuum tube?" he asked.

"I checked some science texts out at the library, trying to get a grasp about what you're doing," she said.

When it dawned on Daniel that she was talking about his project, he urged, "And?"

"And . . . I . . . well, assuming you're going to reflect or refract light—"

"This is so *damned obvious!*" Daniel exploded. Why hadn't he thought about it? Sure, he'd spent hours the past week with his engineers trying to work the bugs out of a computerized planter system, but he'd always been able to handle several projects at once.

Admit it, Daniel, he told himself. So he did. The reason he'd overlooked the obvious answer of a glass tube was that for the first time in his life he had a personal dilemma demanding equal time.

For the next fifteen minutes they talked.

Or Daniel talked. Jill listened while he explored the possibilities of coating a tube with black paint. Plain old soot was the best thermal radiator. Curling irons used a rod. A glass tube painted black held possibilities.

She wanted to understand Daniel. Autry had offered some insights about his complicated brother. Also enlightening was Daniel's statement that his mother had held her own with his father and grandfather when it came to him. It seemed significant because there'd been a pause before he added Autry.

But now, because he was pampering her with his gaze, just as he had pampered her with his kiss and his touch, the issues were confused. Her motives were unclear. Was she here because she knew Daniel was not eccentric, but lonely? Or was she here because it was she who was lonely?

When she was a teenager and her friends Cassie and Abbey gushed about Bob and Travis, Jill would groan that they were being silly. Bob was her cousin. He was likable, lovable, but not much to get rapturous about. And Travis was as likable and lovable as Bob, but Jill

had never understood why Abbey had felt her life
ended when she and Travis broke up. Or why she'd felt
she'd started to live again when she and Travis mended
their relationship.

Always, she would tell them, "Hey! Listen—there
is a life, a world beyond a man."

And Cassie and Abbey had warned her, "You wait.
Someday!"

Jill was not convinced that someday had arrived,
but when her suggestion caused Daniel's eyes to
lighten with enthusiasm, she felt as if she had shared
a special moment with him, contributed something to
his well-being.

And the spark was definitely there. She would be
less than honest if she didn't admit that she would like
to explore *touching* Daniel to a greater degree.

"I can't wait to try it," Daniel said. He straightened. "I'm going to head for the mall right now."

He was moving toward the door. Actually, she, also,
was moving toward the door. He had slipped his hand
under her elbow, assisted her from the stool, then
pulled, guided her along.

By no stretch of the imagination could she read
anything romantic into the gesture. She could have
been a puppy on a leash for all the attention he was
giving her. His object was to get her out of the workshop and gone.

"What are you going to do at the mall?" she asked.

"I need some curling irons," he said. "I'll take
them apart...start constructing a prototype using your
glass tube idea."

Whoops, she thought. Score one for the competition—his work. But there was always tomorrow.
Daniel couldn't spend all of his time working. Even
she didn't spend *all* of her time working.

Chapter Seven

As it turned out, she didn't see Daniel the following day. Nor on any of the following evenings when she dropped items off at the Holiday house. Nor did she see Autry. He and the show girl were having a whirlwind romance. It was the main topic of conversation at the center.

When she arrived on Wednesday evening, Belle came from the house to help her unload the car. After they'd finished and Jill was preparing to leave, Belle said, "Come. Before you go, I want to show you the pen Daniel made for Chester."

Belle led the way to the back of Daniel's workshop. Not far from the double garage doors was the pen Daniel had built using hog panel and steel posts. A small shed, built like a barn, painted red, trimmed in white sat inside the confinement. He had connected an automatic hog waterer to a faucet, dug a hole in the sand and cemented it, providing Chester with the fanciest hog wallow Jill had ever seen.

As a finishing touch, Daniel had set up a second small storage shed outside the pen and supplied it with more pellets, timothy hay and wood shavings than one small pig would use in a year.

"Chester will think he's landed in hog heaven," she said, wondering how much it had cost—more accurately, how long it would take her to pay it off.

Belle laughed. "When Daniel gets going on a project, it's hard to stop him," she said.

"The storage shed is nice, but a bit more than I'd expected," Jill said.

"I suggested you could store Chester's supplies in Daniel's workshop," Belle said. "But Daniel thought it would be more convenient for you to have the pig supplies stored close at hand."

Jill stared at the closed double doors at the back of the building. The lights were on again this evening as they had been every night. She had overextended her last visit, and she believed she hadn't seen Daniel because he had been avoiding her. So it was more likely that he didn't want Chester's things stored in his hideaway because he didn't want her to interrupt him.

"That was considerate," she said. "When I get settled, I'll pay him—"

"Pay him!" Belle said. "He doesn't expect pay. He said something about owing you for giving him an idea."

The rest of the week passed in a blur. Jill and Shauna were finalizing the tours and setting up square dance classes, also to begin in January. The possibility of starting a driver's education class had stimulated interest in other classes. Jill was talking daily with the adult education center, asking about such specialized interests as financial and real estate planning and nutrition. And the list kept growing.

To complicate matters, Hattie had called to tell her that Matthew was refusing the therapy he'd been offered. She asked Jill to come to the hospital to talk to him.

On Saturday evening she managed the visit. She arrived at the hospital to find Matthew sitting in a wheelchair snarling at Hattie about the "poison" she was trying to get him to eat.

Hattie was intimidated at being so totally ineffectual at dealing with her husband. Jill pulled a chair close to Matthew's wheelchair and sat down. It saddened her to see how Matthew had deteriorated in two weeks.

It was not so easy to determine how much of the deterioration was due to the stroke, how much was due to his thorn-in-the-side-of-everyone attitude.

After an exchange of small talk, Jill asked, "How are you really feeling, Matthew?"

He glowered. "How the hell do you think I'm feeling? Can't lift my right leg. Can't lift my right arm. How the hell do you think I'm feeling?"

"Can you lift your left hand?" Jill asked evenly.

"What the hell does that have to do with anything?" he snapped harshly. "I'm right-handed, and don't even think about giving me any crap about taking therapy."

Jill heard Hattie gasp in the background.

"I see that the stroke hasn't affected your sweet disposition," Jill snapped as harshly as Matthew had. "Nor has it affected your ability to think or talk. Your biggest problem right now is feeling sorry for yourself."

"Get out!"

"Make me."

Matthew glowered at her, gritted his teeth. "I've got a right to feel sorry for myself."

"You've got a right to be depressed," Jill countered. "But what about Hattie's feelings, Matthew? Why do you want to make her miserable?"

"Oh!" Hattie interjected. "Matthew doesn't make me miserable, Jill. Don't say that to Matthew."

Jill smiled, first at Hattie, then at Matthew. "How's that for loyalty, Matthew? All Hattie wants for you is a return to your health. And you yell at her about the poison the hospital is giving you."

"I know. I know," Matthew said. His eyes filled with tears.

Jill took his limp hand in hers, rubbed it. "Don't give up without a fight, Matthew. Hattie needs you."

"You're my life," Hattie whispered. She patted his back. "You've got to know that."

Matthew tilted his head up to meet Hattie's gaze before looking back at Jill. "I asked them, if I go for this therapy what kind of chance have I got of walking again? All they said is that the chances are pretty good." He shook his head.

"What will they be if you keep refusing therapy?" Jill asked.

It was late by the time she left the hospital. She was drained emotionally, physically exhausted. But Matthew was going to start therapy and allow a physical therapist to come to the house after he was discharged. He'd also agreed to have Jill look into the possibility of having someone come to their home a couple of times a week to give Hattie a break in her caretaking duties.

Jill was determined to get the driver's education course started. When Hattie knew how to drive, it would give the Duncans more independence.

She was just giving Chester his pellets and making herself a cold meat sandwich when the doorbell rang. She groaned. It had to be Mrs. Chatham, here for one final confrontation. Exactly what she didn't need. An encounter with Mrs. Chatham.

She peeked through the peephole. "Delivery for Jill Fulbright," the young man said.

Jill looked past him to the street. Ulrich Florists? When she opened the door, the young man shoved a long white box toward her. "Have a good evening," he said.

She smelled the aroma of roses even before lifting the lid to find a dozen red roses under the green tissue. The card read, "In brilliance, Venus on the horizon is like the flicker of a candle when compared to you. Daniel."

Did he realize he had written unforgettable words? she wondered. To the point, had he *intended* to write memorable words? She didn't know because she doubted that he realized the powers of his masculinity.

It didn't matter *why* he'd done it. She was going to forgive him his trespasses against her, primarily his managing to avoid her all week. She buried her nose in the roses.

Since she'd moved the two vases she had, Jill emptied the small amount of milk left in a carton and filled it with water. She placed the roses in the carton and set the bouquet in the middle of the kitchen table.

She used a paper plate for her cold meat sandwich, a plastic fork for the small can of pork and beans she was eating cold. But with the aroma of the roses fill-ing the air and the vision of a handsome man sharing the meal, she felt as if she were dining at the snazziest place in town.

Sunday, after church, Jill and Chester moved into the apartment. The welcome was provided by Belle, Nell, Phoebe, Ralph, Autry and Hildi, the Duncans' granddaughter who had flown down to see her grandparents.

Autry grilled hamburgers. The women provided salads and desserts. Jill visited with Hildi, who was charming but superficial. Jill really had expected Autry to be a bit more choosy.

But when Hildi thanked Jill for helping her grandparents, she did it so sincerely that Jill felt guilty about wondering what Autry saw in her outside her body, which was terrifically displayed in short shorts and blouse of hot pink.

Maybe it was her mood. She wasn't feeling as up as she had expected to be feeling. Something was missing. Definitely missing. Daniel had flown to Chicago. And try as she might not to feel it, Jill was frustrated.

Of course, she didn't expect him to neglect his business and work, but he could have said something about being gone on his note. That way she wouldn't have expected to see him.

It was Friday before she did see him. She was late getting home from the center and it was after eight by the time she'd changed clothes. As she went to get Chester, who'd been spending his days in the pen because the temperatures had moderated, she saw that the light in Daniel's workshop was on.

Her pace quickened. She walked around the building, whistling to alert Chester that she'd arrived. But when she got to the pen, his gate was standing open, as were the double doors of the workshop.

She found Chester with Daniel, stretched out on an old towel Daniel had placed on the cement floor. Chester was sleeping. Daniel was working with an elongated tube, using a small, camel-haired brush to paint the inside black.

On the table he had at least twenty more tubes and five or six small cans of black paint. For the first few moments she knew that he wasn't aware of her presence, so she studied his profile, the way his forehead was furrowed in concentration.

Suddenly she realized that he was aware of her silent study.

Her lips started to form the word *hello*, but she didn't utter it. This time, he would break the silence.

"Looking for Chester?" he asked.

Jill smiled. Maybe he had released Chester because he knew she would come looking for him.

She walked to the workbench. "Yes. But it looks as if he doesn't care that I found him," she said. "He's out like a light."

In the workshop corner office, the fax phone clicked in, rolling out a three-page document. Jill turned in that direction. There was a pile of documents on the desk. Daniel ignored the machine.

"Daniel," she said. "Your fax machine. Did you hear it?"

"I did," he said. He held the tube to the fluorescent light suspended over the table, squinted. "Think I've covered the interior, don't you?"

Jill edged closer. She squinted. "Missed a tiny spot—" she pointed to a minuscule spot on the bottom of the tube "—right there."

"It's Chicago," he said.

"What's Chicago?"

"On the fax. I have a company—"

"Autry told me. Belldan," she said. "I hadn't realized all you'd accomplished."

Daniel wished she hadn't said that. Hadn't even thought it. But she was too honest not to have said it. "We're still trying to iron out a small problem with a computerized planter," he said. "I should have stayed in Chicago but I wanted to get on this."

He dabbed the spot she had pointed out.

"Thank you for Chester's pen. It's palatial."

"You're welcome. Chester's welcome."

"And for the flowers."

"You're welcome again."

"The note was wonderful."

The note had been a mistake. An impulsive gesture on his part, Daniel realized. Give a hint that you're vulnerable and someone will take advantage of it.

He looked puzzled. "The note? Oh, the one with the roses?" he asked. She nodded. "Just my way of saying thank-you for nudging me in the right direction."

Jill realized she'd done it again. Edged over the line declaring this far and no farther. But she was sure that when he had written the note he had intended it to be personal. He was hiding his true feelings. But why did he go to such lengths to disclaim any soft spot?

She moved slightly away. "Why the array of paints and tubes?" she asked.

"The tubes will eventually contain the heating element in the curling iron. I hope," he said, not without a smile. He picked up a small can, offered it to her. "You'll see that each of these black paints has been made with various additive mixtures of red, green and blue," he said. "Only by experimenting with each will I know which will be the best thermal radiator."

"And what will supply the heat?" she asked, handing the can back to him.

"The light bulbs are over there on the workbench where the curling irons are sitting," he said.

She walked to the far side of the building to the bench he'd indicated with a toss of his head. The curling irons—what was left of them—were scattered in pieces all over the table surface.

She half laughed. "Destructive little devil, aren't you?"

He laughed. "Only by tearing something apart can you reconstruct it. The bulbs are in a jar to your right."

Jill picked up the jar. "They look like Christmas tree lights—the twinkling kind."

"That's exactly the size," Daniel said. "I don't know right now how many will be necessary to accomplish the results I want...but it shouldn't be more than two."

Sighing, Jill returned the jar to the workbench. She wasn't at all sure he was going to be successful on this one. How could a little bulb like that generate enough heat to curl hair?

By the time she got back to the workbench, Daniel was engrossed in painting a second elongated tube. Not wanting to push her luck, Jill woke Chester by tickling him under his chin. "I have a peanut treat for you," she said softly.

With Chester trotting at her heels, she left the workshop as quietly as she'd come, sure that Daniel wasn't aware she'd gone.

Several hours later, as she left her apartment to return Chester to his pen for the night, the sound of

Daniel's and Autry's laughter drew her in the direction of the pool.

The lights were on, causing an eerie glow as Daniel and Autry churned the water to foam as they swam lengths. Approaching the edge of the pool, she sat and slipped off her tennis shoes, then dangled her feet into the water. She made a deliberate effort not to watch Daniel, who swam at the far side of the pool.

Of course she did, comparing his movement through the water to that of a sleek dolphin. She was becoming a full-blown romantic. But his body was...sleek. It was trim. It was very...male.

Autry bobbed to the surface at her feet. "Hello, good-looking," he said. "How are things going?"

"Dandy," she said. "Just dandy. How's Hildi?"

"Hildi who?" Autry asked. He laughed.

"You're shallow, Autry," Jill chided. "Really shallow."

"You didn't like Hildi," he countered. "I could tell."

"I did like her," Jill protested. "It's just that I wondered what—"

"I saw in her?" Autry laughed. "You're right. I'm shallow. But you have to admit that she looked great in hot pink."

Jill kicked her foot, splashing water in Autry's face. Chester, standing next to her, leaned forward, sniffed the water, snorted and backed away.

"What's his problem?"

"I think pigs instinctively avoid water so deep that they might have to swim," Jill said.

"Come to think of it, I've never seen a pig swim," Autry said. "What's the scoop on your social director?"

"No scoop that I know of," Jill said. "Shauna is young. Attractive—"

"Enough said." Autry laughed. "Phoebe told me I ought to drop in to the center to visit. She said the social director, Shauna, had all kinds of things going for them."

Jill laughed. Now Phoebe was actively in on the plotting. What next? "Well. Are you going to drop by to visit?" she asked.

"Nope," Autry said. "I think it will be a heck of a lot more fun to wait and see what Nell and Phoebe try to come up with next."

Daniel swam toward them, backstroking. When he reached them, he stood. Jill wondered distractedly why she had never noticed how a man looked, raising his arms to run his fingers through his hair.

"Why don't you change into your bathing suit and join us?" Daniel offered. "We'll give you a swimming lesson."

Since Daniel asked, she would have given anything to join him in the pool. However, there was a small complication.

"I don't own a bathing suit," she said.

"You're kidding," Autry said. "Not even one for sunbathing?"

"Nope. And I know that learning to swim is something I should learn to do," she admitted. She splashed her feet. "But this is good enough for me."

"Are you afraid of water?" Daniel asked.

"Not in the least. I love boating, waterskiing—"

"You water-ski without knowing how to swim?" Daniel asked.

"I wear a life jacket," Jill said. "As you can see—" she tapped her chest "—I haven't drowned yet."

Autry laughed.

"The point is," Daniel said sternly, "you could drown in this pool if you fell in."

"The point is— I don't intend to fall in," she countered.

"Daniel's right," Autry said. "You should learn to swim. Let me teach you."

Daniel slid back into the water, rolled over and began to stroke. He hadn't intended to cut in on the conversation Jill and Autry were having. Still, he didn't think he'd cramped Autry's style.

He couldn't cramp Autry's style! Even if he tried. And he wouldn't try. Easy as Jill was to be with, he knew it was best to allow things to stay as they were. Cordial. Easy. No complications. That way he didn't run the risk of feeling left out, rejected.

Chapter Eight

Jill was posting a listing of the tours on the bulletin board when Phoebe and Nell swooped toward her, determination flashing like green lights on their faces.

"Belle says you've gone with her to the flea market the last three weekends," Phoebe said, sounding as if she were accusing Jill of some indiscretion.

"I love flea markets," Jill said, wondering why she was defending herself when she didn't know what crime she'd committed.

"Don't you have anything better to do with your free time than go with Belle to the flea market?" Nell asked.

"We have a ball," Jill countered. "What's your problem?"

"You ought to be dating," Phoebe said. "I have a nephew who is going to visit next week. Maybe you would like to have Thanksgiving dinner with Ralph, Tim and me."

"That's considerate, Phoebe, but I can't," Jill said.

Nell chuckled. "You owe me a quarter, Phoebe. I told you she wouldn't go."

Jill stuck the last plastic-headed tack in place. "Only because I'm flying out on Wednesday at five to spend Thanksgiving at home. I won't be back until late Saturday."

Phoebe laughed. "Got you, Nell. Hand over the quarter."

"She didn't say she'd go if she was here," Nell protested. "Bet's off."

"Oh," Jill said devilishly. "If I was going to be here, I most certainly would go out with Phoebe's nephew. You owe Phoebe, Nell."

"I'll think about it," Nell said. She moved closer to the bulletin board and scanned the tour sheet. "We're still planning on taking cars for the tour to Tombstone in mid-December, aren't we?" she asked.

"Shauna and I thought it would be a better idea than chartering a bus," Jill said. "It would be cheaper all the way around. But if there's an early landing of snowbirds, we can charter a bus."

Phoebe chuckled. "Hattie thinks she'll have her driver's license by then. She says she's going to volunteer her car because Matthew is planning to go alone. It will be his first real trip out."

Jill smiled. Matthew was making a good recovery. He was using a walker around the house, only relying on the wheelchair for trips outside.

Nell made a disdainful sound. "Anyone who gets into Hattie's car has to be crazy," she said.

"Walter Wayland isn't crazy," Phoebe said.

"Walter is the driver education instructor. He gets paid to get into the car with her," Nell countered. "He was white when I saw him after Hattie did the wheelie turning in to the parking lot."

"'Wheelie' is stretching it," Jill said, straight-faced. "So she took out the cactus bed by the street. Anyone who missed the entrance would have done the same."

Nell and Phoebe looked to where Ralph stood visiting with Belle and the man they had been talking about, Walter Wayland. Walter himself was a senior citizen, a retired high school teacher, who was also qualified to teach driver's education. Even the least observant person couldn't help but see that Walter's interest in Belle was more than passing.

"Land," Nell murmured. "Be a shame if Hattie wiped out Walter before he gets the chance to ask Belle out."

Jill, giggling, posted a second notice, this one pertaining to the square dance schedule. Then a third, containing the pairing for the city tennis tournament starting the Friday after Thanksgiving.

"I see you and Ralph play at four on Friday. Again on Saturday if you win," Jill said.

Phoebe nodded. "If we don't win this one, we'll try again in March," she said. "Though the competition will be tougher because all the snowbirds will be in town."

"I'm sure you and Ralph will do fine in the post-Thanksgiving tournament and in March," Jill said. She stuck the last tack in place. "I wish I was going to be around to cheer you on."

"How are you and Daniel getting along?" Nell asked.

Jill smiled. Nell had almost forgotten to ask the daily question. "Fine," she said.

"He's ignoring you, isn't he?" Phoebe asked.

"No, he isn't."

"Yes, he is," Nell said. "We'll just have to see what we can do about that."

Jill was laughing as they walked away. Before coming to the center, she had thought she had never had a boring day. Now the days were not only never boring but they flew so fast that she couldn't keep track of them.

Or maybe they flew because she anticipated the end of each day, anticipated going home because Daniel was there. She knew he wasn't deliberately ignoring her. But most of the time he was holed up in his hideaway paying scant attention to anyone.

They did visit. She knew exactly how he was progressing on the curling iron. But when it came to personal exchanges, much more was being left unsaid than was being said.

She had begun to wonder whether she hadn't imagined he liked her, she liked him. But... Venus on the horizon was a flicker of a candle compared to her....

Bottom line, she was sure of only one thing. She wanted to see more of Daniel than she was seeing. Only by seeing him would she know where she was headed....

Daniel had felt the excitement building all day. He had worked on the prototype of the curling iron for the past three weeks. After nearly three hundred hours, though it was still a bit cumbersome, he thought it was ready for testing.

When he saw Jill arrive after work, he gave her an hour, then went to her apartment and rang the chimes. As soon as she opened the door he said, "I think we're ready to give it a try." He held out the curling iron. "It's charged. Ready to go."

Jill smiled, turned and walked ahead of him toward the dressing room. "Me, too. I'm charged and ready to go."

If Daniel hadn't known her as well as he did, he would have thought, based on her smile, that there was a sensual innuendo in her words.

But she was too straightforward for that. They had managed a workable friendship. Only in his mind had he danced the periphery of a more tangible communication. He had, to this point, dodged the bullet of a repeat of the kissing episode. He felt he had the best of two worlds. Companionship without complications.

A minute later they were standing before the mirror over the dressing vanity. After setting the unit on the vanity, he leaned against it, watching her slowly brush her hair in preparation to curl it.

He had never watched a woman brush her hair. *Engrossing,* he thought, determinedly philosophical. *And sensual.* Now his thoughts were not so analytical. He was moving into areas like *mesmerizing* and *enthralling.*

"Low will turn on one light," he said brusquely. "High, two. High maintains a rather hot temperature. Does your hair curl easily?"

"It has some natural curl," Jill said. "It twists into wild curls when it's wet."

"You'd better start with low," he advised.

She released the iron from its battery pack. "How long will it maintain its heat?" she asked.

"Approximately twenty-two minutes," he said. "I suppose that might not be long enough?"

She picked a thick strand of hair over her ear, clamped the iron in place and rolled it up. "I would think it would depend on the woman, the kind of hairstyle she wants to wear. The hair itself."

Daniel nodded. "I think you'd better test the curl," he advised.

"It's only been in several seconds," she said.

"All right," Daniel said. "It's your hair."

She looked to the mirror, met his gaze in it. "I think I'm the expert in this area, don't you?"

Daniel grinned. "As I said, it's your hair."

She ran the tip of her tongue over her lips, concentrating. A few moments later she said, "Now. Maybe."

She slid the iron from the curl. Rather than the hair dropping to her shoulder, turning up, it hugged her ear. She jiggled her head, watching the curl bounce. She giggled. "I remind me of Nell!"

He reached over, pulled the curl out. When he let go, it snapped back into place. They broke into a spasm of laughter. In the midst of it, something in the nature of what they were doing changed for Daniel. Or he changed.

From laughter he went to an abject yearning that was more frightening than any primitive desire. That panicked him. He didn't trust himself. He could not be with her one minute longer.

"I've got things to do," he said abruptly. "Do you want to work with the iron for a while?"

"Well, sure," she said, the sound of levity lingering in her voice. "But don't you want to watch the results?"

"Take notes," Daniel said, forcing lightness. "You could take it back to Iowa with you. Your mother or one of your friends might like to try it." He backed from the dressing room.

"I'll take it with me to Iowa," she said.

"Have a safe trip—"

"I don't leave for a week."

He chuckled. "Just saying it now in case I forget later," he said.

After he'd gone, Jill leaned on the vanity, gnawing her lip. For some unknown reason he had panicked. *He was absolutely terrified of her.* Had he been treated so shabbily by women that he trusted none of them? Or was it only her?

The flight back from Iowa had taken off from Sioux City on time, but had been delayed in Lincoln forty-five minutes. Jill had spent the time trying to read, but had constantly glanced at her watch, wishing they'd get the plane in the air.

She had loved being home. It was wonderful to be able to visit with her parents to her heart's content and not have to worry that she wouldn't be able to pay the telephone bill. She'd seen Abbey and Travis, Cassie and Bob. And had hugged her little niece, Candy, to death.

She had told everyone about Daniel, had them try the curling iron. She was eager to relay the rave reviews she had gotten, but beyond the news she carried she was eager to see him because she had missed him in a different way than she usually missed someone close to her.

Exactly how missing him was different was not clear to her, but she felt driven to define their relationship. Then she bemusedly pondered whether or not they in fact did have a relationship to define.

It was after nine when the airport limousine arrived at the Holiday house. The house itself was dark, but Daniel had a light on in the workshop. Jill made a quick trip to the apartment to drop off her bags, then decided to get Chester.

But before she did that she walked to the workshop door, stood on tiptoe and peeked in. Daniel was engrossed in something at the far end of the building. Apparently he hadn't even heard the limo arrive and depart.

She looked around, thinking Chester might be with him, but the towel where Chester always slept was empty. She left the window and circled around the building. After she got Chester she would go and say hello to Daniel. If he wasn't interested in seeing her, he would be interested in hearing what her mother and friends had to say about the curling iron.

As she rounded the corner and approached the pen, she whistled softly. When Chester didn't come from the shed, she opened the gate, stepped into the pen and whistled again.

"The game is over, Chester," she said. She bent, peered into the shed, but it was so dark that she couldn't see anything. "I'm back. Come out and let me see you."

She didn't know how long she stood there before admitting he was not in the pen. But panic made her heart pound when she noticed where the sand had been rutted and the hog panel pushed up. Chester was gone.

She knew he wasn't inside the building with Daniel. "Chester," she called as she headed back around the building. "Chester. Come here. You're frightening me."

If he had heard, he would have come—if he was capable of coming. She broke into a run, heading toward the house. The skirt of the flowered print dress she'd worn on the flight wrapped around her legs, and her low-heeled pumps hindered her movement.

He had to be with Belle, she thought even as she remembered that Belle had planned to attend the tennis tournament with Walter and Nell. And the house was dark, so Autry was gone.

She wheeled, ran back toward Daniel's workshop, intending to get him to help her look for Chester. She would never have glanced at the pool except that she heard a gentle splashing, barely audible over her rapid breathing.

The air was cold enough that before she reached the pool she could see the steam rising from the heated water. When she arrived she saw Chester in the middle of the pool, his little legs churning like the blades of a mixer as he tried to stay afloat.

She turned toward the shed, screamed, "Daniel! Daniel!"

That was hopeless. He would never hear her. And she didn't have time to go for him. Pigs didn't swim. Chester would drown. She hurried to the shallow end of the pool.

"Chester!" she beseeched as she slipped off her pumps. "Come to me."

He did turn in a tight circle to face her. She whistled. He did a one-eighty. She yelled, "Daniel! For crying out loud! I need help!"

She had no alternative. She waded into the water until it lapped at her knees and the hem of her dress felt like a weight. "Come here, Chester," she begged.

Chester's head disappeared. He came up shaking his head. Jill moved forward, her hand extended. She was in to her chest. Through her nylons, the bottom of the pool felt slippery.

"Chester, come to me," she said. "Daniel! Daniel!"

"What the hell are you doing?" she heard him ask.

Jill looked to where he was standing. The water seemed to be sucking the air from her body. "What the hell does it look like? Chester's drowning."

"Get out of the pool."

"Don't order me around," Jill retorted. She looked back to Chester, who had come within four or five feet of her. "Come, Chester. Just a little closer."

She reached. What happened next she wasn't sure, but suddenly one foot floated out from under her, then the other. She beat at the water. Bludgeoned it. To no avail. She was tipping, slipping under....

"Daniel! Daniel!"

"Stop screaming in my ear," he said. "I have you."

She felt his arms around her at her waist. She clenched his shirt with her fingers, then more or less crawled up his body and grabbed him around the neck. That threw him off balance. They both went under.

He came up sputtering. "Knock it off, Jill!" She tightened her hold. "Relax!"

Her teeth were chattering. "I . . . c-can't."

"You'd better," he warned. "I'm not sure my leg can hold both of us if you keep fighting me."

Jill went limp.

"Good," he said. He swooped her up, settled her against his chest and pushed through the water to the shallow end of the pool, then set her down.

And not too gently. "Ouch," she muttered.

"Stop complaining," he snapped. He plopped down beside her, slipping from his loafers. "I thought you were smarter than that."

"Stop chewing me out. Stop taking off your shoes! Save Chester!"

"I don't think he needs saving," Daniel said. "Look at him."

Chester had circled the pool, entering the shallow end near them. He sauntered from the pool and shook, freeing his body of excess water.

Jill felt sheepish. "I'm sorry I made a big to-do about nothing. Thank you for the gallant rescue."

"I should have checked on him earlier," Daniel said.

Jill held her hair out of her eyes with one hand while trying to squeeze water from her dress with the other. "You were working," she said. "Thank goodness you heard me calling you."

Daniel tossed the shoe he'd just pulled off aside. He hadn't been engrossed in his work. He had been waiting to hear the sound of the airport limousine, worrying about why she was nearly two hours late in arriving.

Then he'd wondered why she'd only peeked through the window at him instead of coming in to tell him that she had arrived.

"The rescue wasn't gallant," he said. "You weren't cooperative enough for it to be gallant. It was more like wrestling a calf at branding time."

She laughed before turning her attention to Chester. She rubbed him behind the ears, crooned to him that while she was upset with him for escaping his pen and taking a swim, she was happy that he was safe.

"I feel the same way about you," Daniel stated. "Upset with you for not thinking before acting, but glad no real harm came to you."

"I knew you wouldn't stay angry," she said confidently. "Autry and your mother. Nell. Phoebe. Ralph. They all say it isn't basic to your nature."

The material of her dress clung intimately to her body, forming a modest V at the neck—but not so modest that it didn't reveal the whiteness of her breasts.

"I've been thinking and feeling a lot of things lately that aren't basic to my nature," he murmured.

"Like what?"

"Why do you want to know?"

"The more I understand you, the more I understand myself," she said.

"I suppose that makes sense to you," Daniel said. "It doesn't seem especially important to me. I understand myself. I'm fairly sure I understand you—"

"Great," she interjected. "Tell me what you understand about me."

He stuck a finger under her nose. "You're a do-gooder," he charged. "You've decided I've got some problem—like Steve had—and you're determined to help me."

"Okay," she snapped. She was furiously wringing water from her dress. "That's good. Now what do you understand about yourself?"

"In spite of what you think," he said, "I don't give a particular damn what anyone thinks about me one way or another. Never did."

Her hand stalled in wringing the water from her hair. "I think you do. I think you have always cared about what people thought. Even those peers of yours who didn't understand your genius. You felt unpopular, rejected—"

"You're full of it," Daniel said. He ran his hands through his hair, flipping the water from it. "You make too much out of casual conversation. Some people are born to be loners. I'm one of them."

He placed his hand on the cement to push himself to standing. Somehow the placing of it brought his arm in contact with her back. He felt a shudder pass from her body to his.

She seemed to lean into his arm . . . or he pushed against her. And then he was drawing her into his arms, breathing rapidly on short intakes of air into his lungs.

He had denied his loneliness but he drew her closer. He believed in self-control but his heart pounded in his chest, pulsed like a hammer in his head.

Without direction, his thumb traced the art of her cheek and he remembered the curve, the texture, the character and substance of her. He traced the outline of her lips, while the fingers of his free hand kneaded her shoulder, her neck before cupping her head in his hand.

Still, he didn't intend to kiss her. But he did. And the kiss wasn't tentative. It wasn't teasing. Not gentle. He was brash and irreverent. A stereotypical man possessed.

And the only thought he had was not comforting. He was not the man he had been anymore. He had changed. Before tonight, all he had intended was to treat her with respect and tenderness, to share some small part of his existence with her.

Yet, he was unrelenting in kissing her. He demanded, pushing his lips against hers. But when she whimpered, he had the sense to know she wasn't expressing passion. He was hurting her. What a fool.

He released her as abruptly as he had embraced her, reached for his shoes to avoid meeting her gaze. "I'm sorry, Jill," he said. He stood, hovered over her. She looked up at him bewildered. "I'm not normally aggressive," he ended in lame explanation.

"I understand," she said. "It's okay."

"How could you understand?" he asked coldly. "I don't expect you to understand. I'm not playing on your sympathy. Get it through your head. I don't need loving care."

"Everyone needs loving care." She stood, challenging him with her gaze as well as her words.

"The image of you challenging me is like David challenging Goliath," he said caustically.

"You know who won the battle, don't you?" she shot back.

"Sorry I made the analogy."

"What I want to know is why you're sorry you kissed me," she said.

In frustration he fisted his right hand and pounded it into the palm of his left. "You are persistent. I'm not sorry I kissed you. I'm only sorry I wasn't smart enough to invite you to participate."

"What if we tried it again and this time I participated?" she asked.

He half laughed. "Forget it. I've told you before. When it comes to women, my attention span is limited."

"Let me see if I have this right," Jill said, wondering exactly why she was pushing him. "It isn't because you're afraid of getting hurt that you avoid getting involved with a woman. It's because you're afraid of hurting the woman . . . in this case, me."

"Right."

"Daniel," she said gently. "Maybe you haven't met the woman who will love you enough to want to share you with your work?"

"That could be," he said coldly. He stooped, picked up his shoes. "You should have Autry teach you to swim."

"Is Autry's time any less valuable than your time?"

"What the hell is that supposed to mean?"

"Exactly what I said."

"Buy yourself a bathing suit," he said. "I'll teach you myself if I have time."

"I'm not putting money out for a suit unless I get a promise from you that you'll find the time to teach me to swim," Jill countered.

Instead of the defensive retort she expected, he laughed. "You win. Get the suit. Tomorrow night at eight I'll give you your first lesson. And now, you'd better get out of those clothes. There's a chill in the air."

She stood at the edge of the pool watching Daniel walk toward the house. She watched until the door closed behind him. There was a chill in the air, she decided. But there hadn't been when he had kissed her.

The thought bedeviled her. In his gentle moments, what making love with him would be like...

She picked up her shoes, whistled for Chester to follow and, sloshing and slopping, headed toward her apartment.

After she showered, she slipped into her old robe and bunny slippers. She sat on the edge of the bed and dialed the phone. A moment later, Shauna answered.

"Thought I'd check in and see how things went at the center," Jill said.

"Ralph and Phoebe made the finals," Shauna said. She chuckled. "According to Nell, the pride of North Cactus is riding squarely on their shoulders."

"Who is she betting with?" Jill asked.

"Frank McKee for one—"

"The social director at South Haven! Good grief. She's corrupting the whole system."

Shauna laughed. "I have a buck riding on Phoebe and Ralph, myself," she said.

"I've only been gone three days. Heaven knows what kind of shape this place would have been in if I'd been gone any longer," Jill teased.

Shauna asked how Jill's holiday had been. Jill gave her a quick summary, ending with Chester's swim in the pool, including Daniel's saving her but omitting what happened after.

"Did Daniel tell you that Walter ate dinner with them?" she asked.

"No," Jill said. "He didn't. I actually didn't talk to him before my venture into the pool. And after, well, we were wet and about all he did was chew me out for getting into the pool without knowing how to swim."

"That *was* pretty stupid."

"Thanks for the words of support."

"Are you coming to watch Ralph and Phoebe tomorrow?" Shauna asked.

"I don't know," Jill said. "Daniel offered to teach me to swim. We're supposed to have our first lesson at eight tomorrow evening."

"Very interesting," Shauna said. "I wouldn't have guessed that anything would have kept you away from watching Ralph and Phoebe."

Long after they had hung up, Jill pondered the conversation. In the last visit she'd had with Phoebe, she'd said that if Ralph and Phoebe won the first round, she planned to attend the finals. But she'd totally forgotten about it.

And that was very unlike her.

Chapter Nine

After lunch on Sunday Jill went to the nearest mall, in search of a bathing suit. In the first store she tried, she spotted a suit in floral print material and decided to try it on.

As she took inventory of herself in the triple mirror, the saleslady said, "The suit looks great on you."

The flowers were muted blues and yellows. A brighter splash of green hinted at leaves. She should have looked like a flower garden. Instead, she looked as if she were either in the process of dressing or undressing.

"The suit looks like a teddy," she said.

"Most one-piece suits do," the saleswoman said. "But you look charming in it." She touched Jill's shoulder, pointing out the built-up straps. "No chance of slippage—but maybe you'd be interested in trying on one of our bikinis?"

Jill outright rejected that notion. Two hours later, after having been in three more stores and having tried on three bathing suits, she returned to the first store and a few minutes later walked out carrying a package containing the flowered suit and a terry cover.

She explained to Chester where she'd been as she sat on the sofa feeding him peanuts. "Since Daniel is going to teach me to swim, I needed a suit," she said. "It isn't that I'm a prude or anything like that, but I couldn't see myself strolling nonchalantly around in front of him in a bikini."

Chester grunted.

"This suit proved to do more to cover my cleavage than the other suits I tried on."

Chester snorted.

"All right," Jill said. She handed him a peanut. "All the foregoing *was* falsehood. I bought the suit solely because I thought Daniel would like it. So I was being vain. Is that a crime?"

Chester stared her down while he chewed.

"And I know that I should be going to the tennis tournament," she said. "It's totally selfish of me to want to be alone with Daniel."

Chester slipped to the floor, laid his head on his forelegs and looked up at her from under his drooping ears.

"I really do not know why I'm doing this," she muttered. But she did. She was on a campaign. Slogan: Making Herself Difficult For Daniel To Ignore.

She rose, walked to the kitchen. She knew Daniel was in his workshop. Refining the curling iron, no doubt. She stood looking at the phone, tapping her finger on her lip. It would be helpful for him to know what Cassie had said, she decided.

She reached for the phone and dialed the in-house number. When he answered, she said, "Jill here. The curling iron got rave reviews from Mother and my friend, Abbey. Another friend, Cassie, wondered whether a larger tube might not give better results—"

"How about the tubes of various sizes that could be switched like the rod sizes on curling irons out now?" he asked.

Good grief, Jill thought. She hadn't even thrown him by calling unexpectedly. "Sounds good," she said.

By a quarter to eight Daniel was in the bathhouse changing into his bathing suit. Never had a day played time games with him the way this one had. He wanted time to stall, but it flew, carrying him inevitably closer to the moment when he would have to face her again.

After last night it would be impossible to pretend he felt nothing for her, equally absurd to pretend what he felt was purely amorous. It wasn't.

Had it been coincidence that he had been thinking about her when she'd called? It may have been, but for the fact that there'd been scant time when he hadn't been thinking about her.

He grabbed a towel and left the bathhouse. A few laps around the pool might burn off some of the excess energy he was feeling.

She was in the pool, standing knee-deep in the steaming water, her back to him as she watched Chester swim. She was dressed in a flowered swimsuit and all he could think was that the pool had taken on an ethereal garden appearance.

He might have spoofed himself, called himself a poor parody of a romantic, but she pivoted, smiling up at him. He lost it. When it came to Jill Fulbright, he was a dreamer. A romantic.

The misty steam of the pool became the falling mist of a waterfall and he could envision himself alone with her on a tropical isle doing what any red-blooded man would do with a beautiful woman.

He tossed his towel on a chair and slipped out of his sandals, then stepped into the pool and walked toward her. He slipped his arm around her waist, led her farther into the water.

"Lie back in my arms," he said.

"Lie back? Why?"

He didn't blame her for asking. She had to see that the blood in his body was running hot. After last night, why should she trust him?

"I'll pull you into deeper water. When your feet start to leave the bottom of the pool, don't fight it. Allow them to come up. You'll float," he said.

Jill did as he ordered. He supported her. And it was lovely, his holding her. "Don't let go," she said.

"I won't. Any problem?"

With what? she wondered. With the way the water was rocking her? Or with her head resting on his shoulder, while his hands slipped down her back to cradle her waist?

"So far, so good," she said.

"Move your hands slowly, keeping most of the action in the wrists," he said.

Jill slowly moved her hands. The motion did seem to add to her buoyancy. Or was it the consummate awareness of Daniel that caused the illusion of floating? She didn't care. She closed her eyes.

He dropped his hands. She sucked in her breath—he replaced them again. "You were floating, you know. Until you thought about it," he informed her.

If only he knew what I was thinking.

"Don't think about it," he said. "Just go with it."

I'm going with it, Daniel! Oh, boy! Am I going with it! "How can I not think about you sneaking your hands away again?" she said.

His soft laugh whispered in her ear. "You sound like Autry," Daniel said. He chuckled. "He was six when I taught him to float. The water in the spring-fed pond on the farm was never over three feet deep. The kid went wading every day and yet when it came to floating, all he'd say was, 'Don't let go, Daniel! Don't let go!'"

"You assured him that you wouldn't, didn't you," Jill stated.

"I suppose," Daniel said. "I don't know."

Jill forced her eyes open, met his gaze. If desire was an ember to fan, she wanted to fan what she saw in Daniel's eyes. "I know. You've always taken care of Autry, protected him," she said.

"Guessing, or did someone tell you?"

"Autry. He said you were his best friend, his protector."

"I love him," Daniel said. "And I owe him."

"How do you owe him?"

"I don't know that I want to get into it," he said. "It's a part of my life that I don't discuss with anyone."

"Trust me to understand," Jill said.

The lights of the pool, responding to the deepening dusk, came on, flooding their water world with an eerie fluorescence.

His laugh was gruff. "Why should I trust you?"

"I'm trusting you not to let me drown."

"You trust everyone," he said. He combed away a strand of fluid hair from where it had floated over her cheek. "And I would think that after last night you wouldn't trust me."

Jill moved her hands faster when she sensed his hands were drifting away. "You won't allow yourself to repeat that performance."

"You think I'm predictable?"

"Predictable, no," Jill said. "Disciplined, yes. The only way you'd kiss me again would be if I instigated it."

"And you wouldn't."

"I wouldn't trust me if I were you," she said.

He laughed. "And to think I spent the day feeling like a heel for taking advantage of you." He shoved her through the water to arm's length while still supporting her lightly. "Paddle those hands!"

Jill paddled. Suddenly she was free of him, floating without so much as his fingers as a tether. "Wow! I'm floating! Hey, Chester! I'm float—" With a splash, she went under.

Daniel lifted her head from the water. He chuckled while she sputtered and spit pool water. "Overconfidence will get you into a whole bunch of trouble."

Was he warning her about being overconfident in learning to swim? Jill wondered. Or warning her about her attitude toward him?

The rest of the lesson passed in a blissful blur. They laughed, talked quietly, talked not at all. When she had learned to float both on her back and her face, he called a halt to the lesson.

They walked from the pool, Chester coming after them. Daniel reached for their towels, tossing hers to her. Jill dried quickly, slipped into the wrap, then sat on a poolside chair, drying her hair.

Chester shook, then stretched out between their chairs.

"You never told me why you felt you owed Autry," she said.

From the frown passing over his brow, the darkening of his eyes, she didn't expect an answer. He threw the towel over his shoulders, settled on the chair next to her and surprised her by answering.

"Three days after my accident, Dad had a heart attack and died," he said. "Because of me, Autry had to grow up without a father."

Pain was etched in his features, evidenced in the convulsive throbbing of his jaw muscle. "I can understand how—as a child—you might have blamed yourself for your father's death. But it had to have been a tragic coincidence. Your accident. His dying."

Daniel, sighing heavily, leaned back in his chair. He toweled his hair vigorously. "My getting caught in the power take-off killed my father. That is an undeniable fact."

Jill had never felt so helpless. She wanted to take him into her arms, hug him, assure him that he was wonderful in her eyes.

"If you don't mind my saying so, your thinking is screwed up," she said.

"I do mind."

"I'm saying so, anyway. You were twelve at the time of the accident. You had a child's emotional needs," she said. "You needed your father as much, maybe more than Autry did."

The crunching sound of car tires in the driveway distracted him. "Looks as if Mother and Walter are back from the tennis tournament," he observed.

Curses, Jill thought. Just as they were getting somewhere. "Looks like," she agreed. "I talked to Shauna last night. I hear Walter was here for Thanksgiving dinner. Do you like him?"

"What's not to like?" Daniel said. He laughed. "Have you heard him describe the ride to Tortilla Flat with Mrs. Duncan driving?"

"No, I haven't," Jill said. But she shivered just thinking about the drive. The road to Tortilla Flat was treacherous and twisting.

Daniel chuckled. "Walter said she kept taking her hand from the steering wheel to direct his attention to points of interest. He kept telling her, 'Two hands on the wheel, Hattie. Two hands on the wheel.' And she kept telling him, 'Don't worry, Walter. I've got things under control.' Darned if it didn't remind me of riding with you."

Jill smiled. It was nice to know he had thought about her on at least one occasion. A moment later Belle and Walter joined them. Walter pulled up a chair for Belle, then one for himself.

Belle leaned toward Jill. "I missed you," she said. "It's good to have you home."

"It's good to be home," Jill said. "How'd Ralph and Phoebe come out?"

"They won the senior doubles," Belle said. "Imagine that! They should be arriving shortly. I've invited everyone here to celebrate."

Even as she spoke, cars began to arrive. "Who is everyone?" Jill asked.

"Exactly what I was wondering," Daniel said. "It looks like an army on wheels."

Belle chuckled. "Ralph and Phoebe, of course. Nell has her own car. And Shauna. By the way, is Autry home?"

"Haven't seen him," Daniel said.

That was the last thing that made much sense in the ensuing ten minutes. The four of them stood to greet the newcomers. Ralph held a small trophy over his head, waving it triumphantly while Phoebe demonstrated the backhand she claimed had won the game. Nell gleefully proclaimed that they'd shown those old duffers from South Haven a thing or two.

Shauna, toting a small bag obviously containing swimming attire, gazed around murmuring, "Heavens. This *is* heaven."

At the first opportunity Jill introduced Shauna to Daniel. "Your mother's talked about you so much that I feel that I know you," Shauna said.

That his mother had talked about him came as no surprise. That Jill hadn't talked about him to Shauna came as no surprise, either. No doubt she might make a casual remark, but she would never discuss anything said between them. He was sure of it.

"Mother's had some good things to say about you," he said.

"I've never heard Belle make a disparaging remark about anyone," Shauna said. "Though I expect any comment she made was good."

"I heard that," Belle said. She laughed. "The secret is not to get me going, Shauna, dear, you'll find the bathhouse over there." She pointed to it. "Whenever you want to swim, feel free. Now, is everyone swimming or will someone hit a few tennis balls back and forth with me?"

Belle was looking directly at Walter.

"If you have a spare racket around," Walter said, "I'll hit a few."

Belle grinned like a miner discovering pure gold, Jill reflected. "It does so happen that we have spare rackets."

Belle blushed. Daniel nudged Jill in the ribs as if he wanted to make sure she saw it. Shauna left for the bathhouse and Belle and Walter walked with her. The equipment was stored in a small room in the same building.

"Isn't that lovely?" Phoebe asked. "Belle and Walter make such a nice couple."

"Mother's been lonely for a long time," Daniel observed. "It's good to see that she's found someone she enjoys being with."

Nell cranked one of the curls over her ears, purring as she did, "I'm someone, Daniel. Doesn't your mother enjoy being with me?"

Daniel tossed his arm over Nell's shoulder. "Who doesn't enjoy being with you—even if you are out to pick their pockets?"

Jill snickered. Nell turned on her. "I hear you and Daniel had a swimming lesson. How'd it go?"

What a scalawag, Jill thought. "I can float," she said.

"Daniel?" Nell asked with seeming innocence. "How did the lesson really go?"

He laughed. "It went just swimmingly, Nell. Just swimmingly."

Nell candidly surveyed Daniel. "You didn't even kiss her, did you?"

"For heaven's sake, Nell!" Jill exploded. She met Daniel's gaze. "She's teasing."

"I know she's teasing," Daniel said.

"I *am not* teasing," Nell countered. "Daniel, don't frown at me like that. It makes you look the forty you are and me the six-five I am."

"Sixty-five?" Ralph hooted. "Want to make a bet on that, Nell?"

Ralph and Nell exchanged a few barbs while Phoebe chuckled and Daniel seemed entertained. Jill wished the whole bunch would vanish.

Shauna, wearing a one-piece white suit, returned to the pool. The suit accentuated the positives, especially her long, tanned legs. She tossed her towel over a chair, and headed in the direction of the diving board.

As she passed, Ralph whistled. Phoebe looked at him and smiled. "Careful, dear. You know how whistling makes you short of breath."

Shauna laughed. She gestured toward the driveway. "Is that a Lamborghini?"

"My brother, Autry," Daniel said.

"Good-looking car," she observed and continued on toward the diving board.

All at once Jill and Daniel were standing alone. "Nell was out of line," Jill said, looking after the seniors as they entered the bathhouse.

"I'm surprised she upset you," Daniel said. "It was innocent jest on her part."

"I wasn't upset for me," Jill countered. "I thought she was making you uncomfortable."

"Not Nell," he said. "Well, now that the swimming lesson is over, think I'll go change."

"You're coming back, aren't you?" Jill asked.

"I hadn't intended to come back. I was going to do a little more tinkering."

"Can't whatever you're doing wait until tomorrow?" she asked. When he grimaced, she threw her hands up in exasperation. "Go. Do it."

"Don't take a beleaguered tone with me," Daniel said.

Jill knew why her temper was flaring. If Daniel left, the evening's enjoyment would pale. He had warned her that no woman held his attention long, but he ought to have a longer attention span than this.

"Beleaguered tone! I will have you know—"

"Hello, people," Autry said cheerfully. "Who's the gorgeous young lady in the pool with Chester?"

"Go find out yourself," Jill snapped. "I'm talking to Daniel."

"Well, aren't you the cheery one."

Both Daniel and Jill silently stared at him.

Autry threw his hands up in a submissive gesture. "Okay! Okay! I get the picture. You two kids want to have a spat, so have at it."

"Kids!" Daniel exclaimed.

"Geez," Autry muttered. Shaking his head, he jogged toward the bathhouse.

"Now," Jill said. "My tone was not heckling—"

"No. It was beleaguered. As in sounding persecuted—"

"All I was trying to do was *suggest* that you'd enjoy yourself if you stayed," Jill said.

"I'd enjoy myself if I left."

Jill made a growling sound.

"That's interesting," he prodded. "Is there a comment to go with that growl?"

"Yes, as a matter of fact there is! You're afraid that if you stay you might *accidentally* have a good time," Jill said.

"That is *so* sweet," Nell said.

"Where'd you come from?" Jill asked.

"From the bathhouse," Nell said. She grasped at her waist as if pinching an inch, lifting the material of the bathing suit up. "I've got my bathing suit on."

"Then why don't you go swimming?" Daniel asked.

"Are you two having a lovers' spat?" she asked.

"Butt out, Nell," Jill and Daniel said as one.

Chapter Ten

Nell laughed in the face of their mutual pique, then turned serious. "I overheard what Jill said, Daniel. And she's right. You work too hard. It wouldn't hurt you to join us."

"Nell's right," Phoebe said. "You work too hard, Daniel. That's why we've decided you're going to volunteer to drive a car to Tombstone."

"Me?"

"It's just one day," Phoebe said.

"A *whole* day?" Daniel asked.

"A *whole* day," Phoebe said firmly. "So plan ahead to be available two weeks from today. We'll leave the center at eight—it is eight, isn't it, Jill?"

Jill would have come to Daniel's rescue but she was downright enjoying watching Phoebe and Nell work him over. "Yes," she said. "Eight."

"This doesn't sound like I'm volunteering," Daniel said. "It sounds like I'm being shanghaied."

"Oh, Daniel," Jill cooed sweetly. "Phoebe and Nell wouldn't do that to you."

"And you, young lady," Nell said.

"Me?" Jill asked.

"How many other young ladies do you see standing here?" Nell laughed. "While we're talking chicken—"

"Turkey," Ralph entered.

Nell eyed Ralph skeptically. She asked Phoebe, "Is he putting me on? Is it turkey?"

"For someone in the restaurant business all those years," Phoebe said, "why can't you get your fowl straight? Ralph's right. You want to talk turkey."

Nell tossed off a gruff laugh. "Let's talk turkey. It's come to our attention that you and Shauna don't have as much social life—"

"That isn't true," Jill said. "Shauna has a social life."

"When did *you* last have an evening out with a man?" Phoebe asked.

Blast it, Jill thought. She'd fallen right into their trap. Ralph, bless his heart, tried to save her. He placed his arm lightly around Phoebe's waist.

"This is getting a bit personal," he said. "Don't you think? Let's swim."

"In a minute," Phoebe said. "I'm waiting, Jill."

Jill laughed. "You're going to wait for a long time, Phoebe, because it's none of your business."

Phoebc smiled. "We know you haven't been out since coming to the center."

"And that's too long to neglect your social life," Nell said. "All work and no play, dear. Don't you know that makes a woman boring? Isn't that right, Daniel?"

"Very boring," Daniel said.

When he snickered to boot, Jill wanted to kick him in the shin. No, she didn't. She loved his smile, loved knowing that while Nell and Phoebe might think he was agreeing with them, she knew she and Daniel were pitted against the golden-aged Cupids.

"No more boring than a man who does nothing more than work," she said, then addressed herself to Nell and Phoebe. "If and when I need a social life, I'll have it," she said. "In the meantime, why don't you lovely ladies take Ralph's advice and go swimming?"

Ralph offered his arms. Twittering, Nell and Phoebe shared him as they walked into the shallow end of the pool.

Before Jill and Daniel could get into it again, Autry trotted up, tossed his towel on the chair.

"I'm back, if anyone is interested."

"Already?" Jill teased.

"Glad to see that you're in a better frame of mind," Autry said. "You're much prettier smiling than you are grumbling around. So, big brother, who's the young lady doing the fancy dive?"

Jill looked to the board in time to see Shauna executing a swan dive. "Not bad," she said.

"Not bad at all," Daniel agreed. "The lovely woman, little brother, is Shauna Gallagor."

Not bad? Jill thought. Lovely woman? Could she be feeling the hot breeze of jealousy sweeping over her? Not a breeze, she admitted. A tempest. Just because Shauna was lovely didn't mean Daniel had to verbalize it. He could have said, *That's Shauna Gallagor.* That would have been enough.

"This is the social director Nell's been trying to get me to meet?" Autry asked Jill.

"The same," Jill said.

"What kind of a buddy are you not to have told me that she's a beauty?"

"She's also sweet," Jill said. "And nice. So you be nice, Autry, or you'll answer to me."

Autry planted a kiss on her cheek. "Okay, mama. I'll be good." He sauntered down the pool, waited until Shauna swam past toward the pool ladder, then dove, arching cleanly over her body.

"Yoo-hoo," Nell called. "Daniel. Jill. Join us."

Daniel looked at Jill. Why was he thinking he should stay? Was it because Autry, who had spent every free moment with Jill since she'd arrived, had taken one look at Shauna and hadn't looked back? Was he feeling protective of Jill for that reason?

That, maybe. But he thought it went deeper, to things like the sounds of laughter coming from the tennis court. His mother had waited a long time, but he knew she was going to allow Walter into her life.

Or maybe it was Jill; her complexity, her openness. The way she had uniquely woven herself into his life. He had no choice. He was staying.

"Shall we?" he asked.

Jill knew Daniel had asked the question after a mental debate with himself. He wasn't asking, *Shall we join the swimmers?* He was asking, *Do we attempt to discover what we're about?*

"Tell you what," she said, trying for just the right amount of intensity, "what I really want is to be with you. The choice is yours. We can either go swimming or back to the workshop. I promise to sit very quietly. Like a mouse in the corner—"

"Witch," he murmured.

One word had changed her life. Triggered awareness. That elusive combination of desirable ingredients, hitherto unknown to her, she now felt. She was in love. Plainly and simply in love.

And she was sure Daniel loved her, also. Of course, knowing Daniel, he would be slow to admit it. But she was a patient person. Hadn't she waited thirty-three years to meet Daniel?

In the end, they compromised. They sat on the edge of the pool, dangling their feet in the water while the others frolicked. For all the world they looked normal, Jill thought. It appeared they were simply visiting.

But what they were really doing was building a foundation for the future.

"Jill," Shauna said. "Telephone for you. A Sara from Washington."

Sara had called on Monday, saying they were in the process of moving into the house they'd purchased. Jill had expected a call from Sara every day this past week telling her to send Chester.

She'd been dreading it. She loved Chester dearly and hated to see him leave. Shauna handed Jill the receiver and left the office to set up for the square dancers.

"Hello, Sara. How are things going?"

For the next five minutes Jill listened as Sara talked nonstop. The news was a mixture of good and bad. Sara was pregnant but there were complications. She would need to spend a good deal of time in bed. She would like to give Chester to Jill if Jill wanted him.

When she hung up the phone, Jill felt emotionally drained. Of course she wanted Chester. That was no problem. When she moved from the Holiday house, she would simply have to look for a place that would allow her to have him.

It was Sara's pregnancy that troubled Jill. Though Sara had sounded confident that everything would work out, this was Sara's first pregnancy and she was forty.

She was late leaving the center. It was Saturday and she was beginning to begrudge last-minute drop-ins like the woman who'd shown up just as she had been ready to lock the door.

The woman wanted to know about the Care cars—how much each trip cost and who drove. Jill could have given her answers over the telephone had she called.

Whoa, there, she warned herself. It was her job. Her responsibility. Her vocation and career. Why was she feeling set upon? She would still make her nightly swimming lesson. Those were the special hours she and Daniel devoted to each other.

Knowing that Chester would be with Daniel, she went directly to the workshop when she arrived at the Holiday house. She intended to tell Daniel that she was home, then go change into her bathing suit.

Chester was sleeping on his towel, while Daniel was sitting on a tall stool, bent over his lighted worktable. When she stepped through the door he greeted her with a smile.

"Trying larger tubes, I see," Jill said.

"Right. Just finishing the paint job."

"Am I your guinea pig again?" she asked.

Daniel laughed. "Why not? Your hair didn't fall out the first time."

"No. But it took three washings to take the curl out."

"You're stretching it."

"A bit," Jill said. She bent and scratched Chester behind the ears. He grunted, but didn't wake up. "Must have had a hard day."

"He's been busy," Daniel said. "He burrowed under the fence twice to go for a swim. His swimming doesn't bother me, but I'm afraid that someday he might wander away. I added a couple of steel posts to the fence. I think that should keep him in."

Jill climbed to a stool, propped her elbows on the bench and, sighing, dropped her chin into her hands. "Thank you," she said.

Daniel glanced at her, set the tube he was painting aside. She appeared wan. Her usual enthusiasm was lacking. "You're tired."

"Mentally," she said. "Why do people postpone until the last possible moment something they could have done earlier? I declare, I had the key in the door tonight, ready to close, when a woman arrived wanting details about the Care car."

"I don't know. But don't most people procrastinate once in a while?"

Jill smiled. "True. But some people take the trait and work with it like it was a talent." She was thinking about him. When it came to business, he made instantaneous decisions. It was quite another thing when it came to his personal life.

He closed the lid on the paint can. "What really has you down?" he asked. "I know it wasn't getting hung up at the center."

He did know her well, Jill thought. But could she possibly explain without sounding as if she were begging for sympathy?

"Sara called this morning—"

"Ah," Daniel said. "When does Chester have to leave?"

Jill quickly explained the situation in Washington with Sara and her husband, the pregnancy and Sara's need to eliminate extra chores. The gift of Chester.

"I don't understand," Daniel said. "Sara's assured you that everything will be fine with her. And knowing how you love Chester, I'd think you'd be bursting into song. But it isn't happening. Why?"

Jill straightened on the chair. She couldn't tell him what was really bothering her. How Sara's call had reminded her that her own childbearing years were slipping away.

He might think she wanted to be with him for that reason, a potential husband and father. Her only need was to be with him because she loved being with him.

"I guess I really am plain tired," she said. "It's been a long week."

"I'm not buying that," Daniel said. "You're depressed. You're avoiding saying why. Weren't you the one who told me to trust you? Is it one thing for me to trust you and another for you to trust me?"

Jill stood, walked to the end of the bench, turned back to face him. "Sara's forty. This is her first child."

"You said Sara assured you that everything would be okay as long as she took care of herself," Daniel said.

"I'm thinking about myself, Daniel," she admitted. "Sara's call reminded me that I'm thirty-three. I have devoted my life to other people when what I truly wanted was to marry and have a family. Does that surprise you?"

"Nothing about you surprises me," Daniel said. He laughed. "Or maybe I should have said everything about you is so surprising that nothing you do or say surprises me."

"Daniel. This is serious."

"Lord knows, it's serious," he agreed. "But women have complications in childbearing at any age. Just last month one of my engineers had to take an early leave of absence. Something about a blood sugar increase. She's twenty-six."

He walked to her, knuckled her under the chin. "Come on. Smile. You aren't over the hill."

"Yet," Jill said.

"Never," he said. "Smile. A white knight will come along."

She studied his dear face, creased in concern. Darned if he didn't look like a white knight to her, handsome and sexy as all get-out, besides being understanding.

"I never believed in white knights," she said. "Too pragmatic, I guess, but—"

"Same here," he said. "But we're going to have to do something to negate the negative mood you're in. How about a swimming lesson?"

That *was* what she needed, physical contact with him. "Good idea."

"Go get ready. Stick in your sheepskin coat and heavy socks—"

"Sheepskin coat and heavy socks!"

Daniel laughed. "Guess I did omit several important details. We'll see if Mother can baby-sit Chester tonight. Pack an overnight bag—"

"Daniel. This does not sound like a swimming lesson to me."

"Call it an overnight camping-swimming therapeutic bound-to-make-you-feel-on-top-of-the-world session. We'll go to my cabin," he said. "Up there, the air is rarefied, but the sky is close enough to touch."

"I hesitate to mention this in the face of your unbridled enthusiasm," she said. "But I heard this

morning that there was a light snow in the area of Sedona.''

Daniel was turning out lights. ''I mentioned your
jacket and heavy socks.''

Jill whistled for Chester. He responded slowly, but
at last stood and stretched. ''I was wondering about
the swimming lesson part. Do you have an indoor
pool?''

''Sort of,'' Daniel said.

Jill lay back with her eyes closed. The warm water
of the whirlpool swirled around her. Some *cabin*. An
A-frame with redwood beams, balcony. Four bedrooms, four baths and the kitchen-family room. Absolutely what no one would call roughing it.

''I'm showing signs of decadence,'' she murmured.
She slipped her feet across the bottom of the whirlpool bath, nudged his leg. ''Hey, you. Are you sleeping?''

He laughed. ''I thought you were. At least your eyes
have been closed for the last five minutes. You call this
self-indulgence?''

''When you asked me to choose between a dip in the
creek where the ice was beginning to form or the
whirlpool, I chose the whirlpool. Definitely a sign of
decadence.''

''Maybe not,'' he said, his voice sounding a tease.
''Maybe it's a sign of old age.''

''Old age? My foot to you, mister.'' Jill played her
toes over his leg.

He chuckled, but she felt the contact weakening her
physically in a way that the slushing warm water
hadn't. She withdrew her foot. It was safer that way.

''Feeling better?'' he asked.

''I'm feeling better.''

"No residual gossamer ties binding you to depression?"

"No gossamer ties."

He stood, extended his hand to her. "Then we're up and out of here and on to stage two."

Jill took his hand, allowed him to pull her upright. "Stage two...for heaven's sake, don't tell me that you're going to ask me to take a dip in the stream!"

"Nope," Daniel said. "Something better."

He lost his train of thought. All he wanted was to touch the explosion of ringlets that had been formed in her hair by the steam. But in his present frame of mind, to touch would mean loss of self-control. And he did not want to deal with the aftermath of that.

He stepped from the tub, grabbed a towel, handed her one as she climbed out. "Did I ever tell you that I like that bathing suit?" he asked.

"Nope," she said. "But on the first night I wore it, I saw that you did."

"Really?"

"Really. Your eyes said, 'Wow. Jill looks okay.'" She laughed. "What's stage two of this operation?"

"Stargazing."

"Sounds like a winner to me," Jill said. And after that was he planning a stage three? She could hope.

It was a half-mile hike from the cabin up the mountain to the place Daniel told her that he always went when he wanted to stargaze. There had been snow, but it was light and their boots kicked it up with each step.

She was wearing her sheepskin jacket with its huge collar. She could turn the collar up to protect her ears should she get cold. But that was unlikely. Before Daniel had allowed her to step into the night, he'd insisted that over her blouse she slip on one of his flannel shirts.

Daniel set a healthy pace in climbing. By the time they had arrived, in spite of the light snow and brisk air, she was feeling cozily warm.

He double-folded the blanket he had brought along and spread it on the ground. Jill sat. She pulled her legs up, wrapped her arms around them.

Daniel settled beside her, turning up the collar of his heavy plaid jacket. "No comment about my farmer jacket?" he asked.

"I like the brightness of it," she said, feigning deep, studious reflection. "But it looks more like a hunter's jacket to me."

"I haven't hunted in years," he said seriously. "I was sixteen when I shot my last buck. I hated myself for doing it. He was a magnificent animal."

"Why did you hunt if you hated it?"

"Meat for the freezer," he said. "The farming operation was going through a bad time. We'd had a poor crop due to drought. The twenty-four head of fat cattle we had ready to sell would pay what we owed on the elevator and the semiannual taxes, providing we didn't keep one of the steers back to butcher. It was that close. So the buck ended up feeding us through the rest of the winter."

Jill studied his profile as he talked. "I feel badly that you had to go against your personal convictions," she said.

"I had a strong motivation for compromising. Grandfather Holiday was after Mother to sell the farm to him. He was sure we'd lose it otherwise," Daniel said. "Life takes some strange twists. A few years later he lost his shirt. It was with no small degree of pleasure, I assure you, that I was able to give him the money to bail himself out.''

Something else about Daniel had been clarified. How on the one hand he seemed put off by money, or the display of it, while on the other hand he was so industrious in making it.

''You've done it all of your life, haven't you?'' she said. ''You've sacrificed something of yourself to provide security for your family. And put your personal life on hold.''

He laughed. ''That's too noble. I did what I had to do to provide. As for my personal life, I think you guessed it. The right woman just never came along. Now why don't we do what we came to do. Let's look at the stars.''

''Right,'' Jill said. She snuggled closer to him. ''How about sharing body heat?''

He slipped his arm around her, tucking her in, then tilted his head back to gaze at the sky. He chuckled. ''It's hard to believe we're rolling in space at a thousand miles per hour.''

''It's a wonder,'' Jill agreed.

''A person doesn't often think about the size of the universe during the day,'' he murmured. ''But at night you get a sense of the immenseness of it.''

''In-fini,'' Jill murmured as she looked for Cassiopeia.

''Infinity,'' Daniel agreed. ''Unfinished. Black holes. Distant galaxies. It makes me feel—''

''Reverent,'' Jill interjected.

''Yes. Reverent,'' Daniel agreed. He chuckled. ''Also humble, when I consider there is a distant cluster of galaxies that has more than a trillion stars in it and our galaxy has a paltry three billion.''

Jill impulsively slid her arm around his waist, hugged him. "I don't feel humble at all. Out of all the infinity we can see, out of all of it that we can't see, the wonderful, marvelous thing is that we're sitting here together," she said. "Don't you agree?"

He kept looking to the heavens. She squeezed harder. She wanted an answer. "Don't you?"

Chapter Eleven

"For being no more than two specks in the grand scale of the universe," he said slowly, "I suppose you could say it is pretty awesome that we settled here."

"Awesome, Daniel?" Jill laughed. "Why not something like—it was our destiny?"

"I don't believe in destiny any more than you believe in white knights," he said. "I'm too pragmatic."

"You're right," she said slowly. "We scoff at the world! At all those couples who are stargazing at this very moment and who are dwelling in la-la land. Aren't we the lucky ones!" she teased. "No white knights for us. No princesses needing rescuing."

"We're stuck in the ugly clutches of reality," he chimed in.

"And *ain't* it a blast, Daniel?"

They chuckled, then worked into uproarious laughter.

Jill was free of the panic she'd felt through the day. Life could not be rushed. The living of it couldn't be rushed. You took one step at a time. Savored one emotion. What she was feeling now...

Daniel thought it best to listen for the sounds of the night. But all that came through was the sound of Jill's steady breathing. She had become vital to his universe. No lying to himself about that. He was lovingly trapped by the exquisite light, but tenacious web of her being.

The loneliness that had been tolerable before would be unbearable now. So there was no going back to the way he had been. In spite of the arguments he had so carefully tended against why they should be together, he didn't have a choice. He could only go forward.

They charted the sky, alternating as they named constellations. It became a heated competition, each trying to outdo the other. Eventually the muscles in his leg began to ache. He rubbed it.

Jill noticed. "I'm getting a bit chilled. Ready to go back to the cabin?" she asked.

When Daniel nodded, she jumped to her feet, extended her hands to help him up. "What's this," he grumbled playfully. "Treating me like one of Nell's old duffers?"

"That is your self-concept," she said. "Not mine. I'm feeling younger than springtime."

Daniel moaned. "That's the thanks I get for chasing your blues away?"

They were laughing as they started down the mountain trail, walking arm in arm with the blanket tossed over their shoulders.

Once inside the cabin, Daniel asked, "Would you like to fix us a butter and rum while I start a fire? In-

gredients are stored in the cupboard next to the refrigerator.''

Jill nodded, pleased that he'd felt comfortable
enough to ask her. He was crouched before the fire,
adding shavings to get it crackling, when she came
from the kitchen area with two steaming cups.

She set the cups on the end table next to the sofa,
kicked off her loafers and curled up in the corner.
When Daniel straightened and turned to join her, he
grimaced then turned it into a smile.

His leg was still hurting, she thought, but made no
comment. She handed him a cup, took the second for
herself. For a long time they contentedly sipped and
studied the pictures formed by the flickering flames of
the fire.

Occasionally Daniel would lean forward, reach
down and knuckle the calf of his leg. Finally Jill could
not stand watching any longer. She set her cup aside.
A moment later she was on her knees before him.

"Let me see if I can massage out the knots for you,"
she said. She started rolling up his jeans.

His hand stalled hers. "Forget it," he said.

She patted his hand playfully in a "there, there"
way. "Trust me."

He laughed. "Do you really know what you're doing?"

Whether or not he could read what she was thinking, the question was germane. She was following her
heart.

"Heaven's sake, Daniel," she said. "Of course I
know what I'm doing. I was going to be a sports
trainer before I went into social work. Never got beyond the first aid level, but what the heck, stick that
leg out here.''

In one quick motion she sat, shimmied closer to the sofa, tucked his sock-covered foot in her lap and began gently kneading.

Eventually he relaxed, laid his head back. "You do know what you're doing," he murmured.

Jill wondered whether the contact was doing to him what it was doing to her. She was warming and it wasn't due to the fire at her back, or to the buttered rum.

She had better concentrate less on the texture of his skin and the sensual nature of her flush. Conversation was good. Conversation was *always* good.

"Tell me more about your father."

"Dad? What do you want to know about him?"

"Tell me about your relationship with him," she said.

"It isn't important," he said.

Muscles that had begun to loosen tightened beneath her fingers. She massaged with greater force. "Your body tells me that it is important," she stated in a matter-of-fact tone.

He half laughed. "Body language now?"

"Did you love him?"

Daniel sighed so heavily that she both heard and felt the tremor. "You should have asked if he loved me," he said. His laugh was curt, filled with self-ridicule. "But I have to admit that I wasn't an easy child to love. How many fathers get a call from the superintendent when a kid is in the first grade, telling him the kid is gone? Just walked out."

"Not many," Jill said. She rolled his pant leg down, eased from the floor to the sofa and sat sideways facing him, one leg curled under her. She leaned with her left arm on the back of the sofa. "So why did you skip school?"

"I remembered a rock I'd spotted at the bottom of a spring-fed stream that meandered through our pasture," he said. "It sparkled under the water. And I got to wondering what would happen if I hit it with a hammer. So I left school and went to get the rock so—"

"You could hit it with a hammer," Jill ended. She chuckled. It was impossible at that point to keep her fingers from touching his hair. "Soft as silk" was a romantic cliché, she thought. But his hair was soft as silk.

She knew touching was bonding. And she desperately wanted to bond with Daniel, so she allowed herself to caress.

"Certainly after you'd explained to your father why you'd wandered away from school, he understood," she suggested.

"Understood? Never," Daniel said. "I was an embarrassment. The *imperfect* child. The daydreamer. All I ever heard from him was, 'Just stop daydreaming. If you're as smart as everyone says you are, that ought to be easy enough.'"

Jill slipped her free hand toward him. He reached for it, then grasped it so tightly she had to fight to keep from grimacing. She wondered at herself. She truly felt hate for a dead man because he had caused so much mental anguish for Daniel.

"What about your mother? What did she do?"

Daniel laughed. "Told me what a wonderful, lovable and brilliant child I was . . . but she was Mother."

"And you wanted the respect of your father," Jill stated. "Did he actually call you imperfect? An embarrassment?"

He thought for a minute. "I'll have to admit that I don't recall him saying that. Only Grandfather saying it, and Dad not defending me."

"Well, turning off your wonderful visions would be impossible," Jill stated. "Didn't anyone ever explain that to your father?"

His fingers entwined in hers. "The school psychologists and the teachers tried. Lord knows, Mother tried, too. His answer was always the same. 'I'm only doing what's best for Daniel. If he doesn't stop daydreaming, someday he's going to hurt somebody.' "

His voice wearied, drifted away. His gaze came to meet hers, unveiled. Hostility, anguish, aching—all were there. So were unrequited love and rejection.

Now it was easy to guess what had happened the day of the accident. "You were daydreaming the day of the accident," she said softly. "About what?"

Daniel half laughed. "A unicycle I was putting together in the workshop."

Daniel saw it in the dark depths of her eyes. She knew he was feeling the full spectrum of emotions for the first time in his life. Had she also guessed that while he was not totally inexperienced in the physical aspects of making love, he was naive when it came to the sensitive art of making love to a woman he loved?

Because he had never been in love before.

She rested her head trustingly on his shoulder. Her hair formed a golden pond on his chest, rippling waters as he breathed. Her fingers twined in and out in his, not demanding, but accepting.

He shifted his weight to lean over her, groaned as he engaged the fingers of his free hand in her hair. "You should stop this," he whispered.

"Stop what?" she asked.

"You've been warned," he said.

"Duly warned." She adjusted herself, began un-buttoning the heavy shirt he was wearing. "I need to be close to you, feel the warmth of your skin as you hold me."

He slipped free of his shirt and dropped it to the floor. Then he unbuttoned the flannel shirt she was wearing. But his progress was hampered. Her fingers were splayed on his chest, fire branding.

Out of the chaos of thought, he murmured, "You looked cute wearing this."

"With the sleeves rolled up to my elbows? Cute?"

She kissed his shoulders. Branded again. "Cute." He tossed the shirt aside. He'd forgotten she was wearing the jersey blouse. "Damn!"

She sat, laughing. "It was your idea," she said. "Your shirt over my blouse."

When the blouse disappeared, Daniel took a long moment to study the flawless beauty of her body. Then he drew her to him. At the first contact of skin on skin, his breath caught. This was like nothing he'd experienced.

He kissed the top of her head, teased himself with the feel of her hair slipping through his fingers. He was feeling possessive, yes, but now the tenderness was paramount.

She tilted her head, gazed hard into his eyes, raised her hand to cup his chin. She traced his lips with her fingertip. Without lowering her hand, she kissed him. . . .

"I'm not this brazen," she whispered.

"Your breath is hot, moist. Sweet."

"It must be the buttered rum," she said.

She was precious, he thought. "Are you sure it isn't me?" he asked. He lowered her hand, took it to his heart, held it there. "I was hoping it was me."

"It is you. First and exclusively. Only you."

It took him a moment to realize what she'd said. "God, Jill. How I love you," Daniel groaned. "If only . . . I knew what the future held."

"My friends," Jill said, her voice sounding sluggish, "told me that someday I would meet a man and from that moment on life and love would be synonymous. Now I know what they meant. I've found you. You are my love. I have no fear of the future."

There were no more words between them. He locked her in a warm embrace, and they slept.

Six cars were lined up in the parking lot as the seniors prepared for the trip to Tombstone. Drivers were Daniel, Autry, Shauna, Ralph, Hattie and Walter, who was a last-minute replacement for Jill, whose car had had a nervous breakdown the day before. Or something. At any rate, according to Daniel, it spit transmission fluid every time she tried to shift.

Autry had offered to drive her to work the previous morning. No surprise. The romance between him and Shauna was heating up and neither was making an effort to hide it. Autry had spent half the day at the center. Shauna had driven Jill home, barely stopping to let her out. Shauna had no time to visit. She had to rush home to change. She and Autry had a date at eight.

In the past three weeks, Jill and Daniel had spent considerable time together when he was home. But he had been gone more days than he'd spent in Mesa. He'd flown to Chicago for four days. And to Florida to make a presentation for the baby-bottle warmer he'd developed.

They were in love. Deeply and irrevocably in love.

But Daniel had a private war going. There was some buried secret yet to surface. At this point, all Jill could do was wait for him to spill it. And then, hopefully, they could start making a few plans.

Otherwise, everything had been going swimmingly, thank you. Until now.

There were twenty-eight seniors needing rides. Of those, twenty-six had expressed the sentiment that they would prefer not to ride with the Mad Hatter, Hattie.

Jill drew Nell, Phoebe and Belle aside. "Someone has to ride with Hattie besides Matthew and me."

"Are you looking at *me?*" Nell asked. She glanced over her shoulder to where Daniel was leaning on the side of his car talking to Shauna and Autry. "Why not have Grace Elliot? I'm sure she'd switch from Shauna's car."

"So you won't ride with Hattie," she said.

"I didn't say that," Nell countered. "but I'd rather ride with Daniel."

Jill counted off on her fingers the seniors who had already asked to ride with Daniel. She slapped her hand on her hip. "I feel like a preschool teacher trying to line up a bunch of unruly kids for a trip to the firehouse."

"I'll bet fifty cents Hattie will get lost between here and Tombstone," Nell said.

"I'll ride with Hattie," Belle said. "That will even things up a bit."

"Walter isn't going to appreciate that," Phoebe said. "But if Nell and I go with Hattie, then Grace and Bill could switch into Shauna's car and—"

Jill threw her hands up. "Whatever. Let's get moving."

In the end, Jill was exactly where she'd wanted to be, riding with Daniel. She had the Cupids to thank for it. They'd wrangled until they managed it.

But Daniel and Jill didn't manage much conversation because Elizabeth Pringle, a nonstop talker, rode in the front seat between them. And she had started talking the moment they'd pulled from the parking lot.

Occasionally Elizabeth made conversation across the back of the seat to Irene Cromber, who rode between two brothers, Tom and Lee Corbeil.

In spite of her chatting, it was Elizabeth who spotted Hattie's green sedan turn left in Tucson instead of right. "Did you see that, Jill?" She pointed to the rearview mirror. "That Hattie's gone back to Apache Junction or to Globe or Lord only knows where—they could get lost in the mountains. Or the desert. And with Matthew in the kind of condition he's in— Daniel, don't you think you should do something?"

Daniel opened his mouth to say no, but the woman was off talking again. He wondered how such a little woman could say all that in one breath. Basically, he simply wished Jill was sitting next to him. He didn't like any distance between them.

He leaned forward, caught Jill's attention, smiled, rolled his eyes toward Elizabeth as if to question whether the woman was real. Jill's lower lip quivered. He smothered a laugh.

From the back seat, Irene said, "Hattie won't get lost. Belle's with—"

"Oh, right," Elizabeth said. "Nell, Belle and Walter—no, not Walter. He's driving. Who is with Hattie?"

When Elizabeth cranked her neck around to hear Irene's answer, Daniel leaned forward again, mouthed, *Does she expect an answer?* Jill mouthed back, *No.* And *I love you.* He smiled, mouthed, *Me, too, you.*

Jill leaned back in the seat, adjusted the seat belt on her shoulder. In the rearview mirror Hattie's car reappeared, swinging in, swinging out as she passed the slower-moving cars on Interstate 10.

Daniel had never set eyes on Hattie and Matthew Duncan until this morning. Then it was a quick introduction made by Shauna. Hattie was a small woman, around sixty, he guessed. Matthew was older. In his seventies, probably.

When Hattie passed them, Daniel commented, "She's doing seventy-five. Wonder what Walter will think when she flashes past him?"

"My goodness," Elizabeth said. "Isn't it wonderful? Walter and your mother. He calls her the Mad Hattie, you know."

Daniel smothered his laugh in a cough.

"Mad Hatter," Irene corrected from the back seat. "Walter calls Hattie the Mad Hatter. Not Belle."

Elizabeth wrenched around in the seat to confront Irene, a plump woman who looked squeezed riding between the brothers. "That was *exactly* what I said," Elizabeth said.

As Hattie passed them, Nell leaned toward the window, a big smile on her face. She pointed to Jill.

"Did you make a bet with Nell?" Daniel asked.

"Fifty cents," Jill said. "She bet me Hattie would get lost on the way to Tombstone."

"You should know better than to bet with Nell," Daniel teased.

"I should know better than to do a lot of things that I do," Jill countered. *I will never regret our weekend in Sedona.* "But sometimes it's out of my control."

"Nothing is ever out of a person's control," Daniel said. *I love her. I'm out of control.*

"Irene!" Elizabeth exclaimed. "Did you hear that Tootie Adams is moving back to Washington? Now if that isn't a foolish thing to do. All comfy and cozy here in the valley and she's moving to all that snow. Well, I never!"

I never, either, Daniel mouthed to Jill.

She smiled. *Relax,* she mouthed. *Just go with the flow.*

Daniel offered a dubious expression. The only way he could go with the flow and enjoy himself was if he had her alone.

After approximately two and a half hours, they pulled into Tombstone and found a parking spot not far from Boothill Cemetery on the north edge of town.

As Jill slid from the car, Elizabeth said, "The Dragoon Mountains are over there. That's where Cochise had his stronghold. And that's Sheepshead. And I just love this place, doesn't everybody?"

There was a chorus of "Sure, Elizabeth."

"Are we going to stop at the Lucky Cuss?" she asked.

Before Jill could answer, Elizabeth had taken off. Jill walked around the car to where Daniel stood, stretching after the long drive.

"Was the woman ever married?" he asked in a low voice.

Jill made sure that the seniors had walked from the car to join the others before saying, "Yes. Elizabeth was married. Four times, as a matter of fact."

"You're kidding," Daniel said. "Four times! I'd never have guessed there would be that many men who would put up with all that talk."

Jill's eyes narrowed. "Listen up, friend," she said. "Elizabeth talks to hide the loneliness she feels—just like someone I know tried to hide his loneliness behind work."

"I've had my hand slapped," he said. "Now would you like to make me feel better by holding it?"

"I'd love to, but Nell bet me a quarter that before the day was out, you and I would smooch—"

"You're kidding!"

"I am not kidding," Jill said. "Nell's already up a quarter on me. If I let her win another, I'd never hear the end of it." She smiled invitingly. "However, we can walk close...and later this evening when we're back home, we can *smooch* to our hearts' content. Or until you lose interest and say, 'Golly, gee, hon. Guess I'd better run.'"

"I have never said golly, gee," Daniel said. "Or called you hon." He gave her a playful boot on the posterior.

Nell called, "I saw that!"

"Doesn't count, Nell," Jill called back. "Open-handed!"

"What doesn't count?" Elizabeth asked.

"Oh, Nell and I are being silly," Jill said. "It's nothing."

Elizabeth pouted. "No one ever tells me anything."

Jill would have comforted the woman but she noticed that Hattie, Shauna and Autry were setting up Matthew's wheelchair and not having much luck doing it.

"Excuse me, Elizabeth," she said. "I'd better see if Hattie needs some help getting Matthew into his wheelchair. Daniel?"

"Right behind you," he said.

They arrived to find Matthew turned in the passenger seat, his legs out of the car, his hand on a four-legged cane. He greeted them by saying, "That wheelchair's nothing but a cantankerous monstrosity."

"I'm going to get it, yet," Autry said. He jerked and pulled to release the wheels. One wheel sprang free, the second didn't.

Matthew laughed. "Can't ride sideways, Autry. Give it up. I'll walk."

"This is an all-day jaunt," Shauna said. "And your first day out. Better ride, Matthew, if Autry can get the thing to run."

"Maybe Daniel could help," Jill suggested.

"Good idea," Autry said. "If Daniel can't get this rig operational, no one can."

Everyone moved aside to allow Daniel to take over. The chair was canvas, chrome and bolts. He thought it shouldn't be as complicated as Autry was making it appear.

Hattie wrung her hands. "It always gives us trouble but today it seems worse. That little gizmo—" she pointed to a lever "—that's what's supposed to pop everything loose."

"No problem," Daniel said. He pushed, he shoved, and adjusted. And the wheelchair fought him. Without looking up, he said, "Autry. Maybe with both of us pulling . . ."

"Sure thing," Autry said.

With Autry on one side and Daniel on the other, they more or less forced it into the shape of a wheelchair.

"Looks good to me," Matthew said. He pushed himself from the car and, using his cane, walked to the chair. He waited until Hattie held it steady, then sat, propping his cane on his leg.

Shauna and Autry wandered off. Jill and Daniel waited until Hattie was ready, then the four followed the rest of the group down Allen Street.

Women of the night, dressed in bright-colored silks and satins depicting an earlier era, and tinhorn gamblers dressed in bright checks and stripes milled amidst the tourists on the sidewalk.

The group visited the Tombstone Repertory Theater and witnessed the shotgun wedding a young couple had arranged. It was hilarious but touchingly beautiful because the couple was so obviously in love.

Nell sidled up to Jill. "You might consider doing something like this yourself, dear," she said in a stage whisper. "It might be the only way to get Daniel to the altar."

Laughing uproariously at her own joke, she left to join Belle, Walter, Ralph and Phoebe as they walked toward the O.K. Corral. The group arrived in time to get a good viewing position for the enactment of the shoot-out between the Earp and Clanton gangs.

When the shooting was over, Doc Holliday, Morgan and Virgil Earp lay wounded. Frank and Tom McLowery lay on the street dead while Billy Clanton had died draped over a hitching rail.

As the dust settled, Elizabeth started wailing, "Oh, my Sanford! They've killed my Sanford!"

It happened so quickly that Jill would never be able to explain exactly who said or did what next. All she knew was that when she realized Elizabeth intended to run to where a young man was draped over the hitching rail, she slipped her arm around Elizabeth's waist and held her back.

Someone asked, "Who's Sanford?" Someone else said, "Elizabeth's first husband." It was obvious to everyone that Elizabeth was convinced that the "dead" outlaw was Sanford. Nell, Phoebe and Belle formed a protective cocoon around Elizabeth and Jill.

"This is pretend, Elizabeth," Nell said soothingly. "That isn't Sanford. Just a young man playing dead."

"Sanford died in World War Two," Belle said. "Remember, Elizabeth? You have the Purple Heart he was given. Remember? You've shown it to me."

"Oh, my, yes. Sanford did...didn't he?" Tears welled in Elizabeth's eyes. "Sanford got shot a long time ago. But...but I'm confused. I really should go to him. I was so angry with him—he just went and signed up. Never asked me. So I didn't tell him I loved him." She looked around Belle to the fallen outlaw. She struggled in Jill's arms. "Let me go! I've got to tell him."

Belle, Nell and Phoebe exchanged looks of concern. Jill said, "But you did tell him, Elizabeth."

"I did?"

"Of course you did," Jill said, trying to think fast. "Remember all the letters you wrote to Sanford—"

"I did, didn't I?" Elizabeth said. "I signed every letter, 'Love, Bethie' and strung kisses at the bottom."

"That's right," Jill said. "Feel better?"

Elizabeth nodded, then contradicted her affirmation by saying, "I don't know why I'm so confused."

Belle smiled. "Too much excitement in one day."

"Belle's right," Walter said. "Too much excitement."

Phoebe patted Elizabeth's shoulder. "You'll be fine in a minute."

"Look, Elizabeth," Ralph said. "Everyone is getting up."

He pointed in the direction of the hitching rail. The cowboy, dressed in a denim shirt and jeans, was brushing his jeans off with his cowboy hat.

Elizabeth murmured, "Oh, my." She started to cry again. "He doesn't even look like Sanford. I don't know what's happening to me."

"There, there," Jill said. She hugged the tiny woman to her. "Let's go across the street to that bar and get something cold to drink."

"Root beer," Elizabeth said.

When Jill looked in Daniel's direction, he nodded to indicate he'd be along. Nell, Phoebe and his mother, understanding Elizabeth's unhappiness, had rushed to comfort her. All were mothers, he was thinking. And widows.

But it was Jill who had comforted Elizabeth with physical contact. With the magic of her touch…which he knew so well. Elizabeth had confirmed what he'd been thinking. There was only one true love in a lifetime. If he messed up with Jill…

"The way that girl manages to get through to people amazes me," Hattie said.

Daniel nodded. Jill seasoned every moment, enhancing it to the point where a person could savor it. "She knows what she's doing, all right," he said.

"That she does," Matthew said. "Just a couple of months ago I was ready to pack it away until she ripped into me."

"Ripped into you?" Daniel asked.

"Turned into a real tiger," Matthew said. He laughed. "Back then, I couldn't raise my hand or move my leg, and she told me to stop feeling sorry for myself. That only being sixty-two, I had a lot of living to do."

"She was right, wasn't she?" Hattie said.

"A lot of living provided you don't wrap us around a pole someday," Matthew said. He grinned up at Hattie. "Think I'll get a governor put on that car."

Daniel didn't hear the rest of the conversation. Sixty-two? Matthew Duncan was sixty-two! Jill wanted children. It had been her plunge into depression when she thought her childbearing years were ending that had sent her rushing into his arms for comfort.

If they married, if they had children, he would be sixty by the time their first child reached college age. Sixty.

His father had died at forty.

God, he didn't know what he'd been thinking. They were too different. Jill wanted to mother everyone. Maybe that's why she'd fallen in love with him, but even that didn't matter. Loving was not enough. He wouldn't risk leaving her alone to raise children.

Chapter Twelve

Autry and Shauna joined him. "You're too deep in thought, brother," Autry said. "There?" he asked, gesturing to where Jill, with her arm still around Elizabeth's waist, was guiding the woman across the intersection. "Or here?" He tapped his head.

"In *your* mind?" Daniel forced a laugh, trying to dig himself out from under the crushing emotions he was feeling. "Never in your mind, little brother. Never."

Laughing, Autry and Shauna moved on to Hattie and Matthew. Autry said something to Hattie. She moved from behind the wheelchair and Autry took over pushing. They followed the rest of the group in crossing the street.

Halfway across the intersection Shauna called back, "Aren't you coming, Daniel?"

"Sure," Daniel said. He joined Jill and Elizabeth in time to hear Elizabeth say, "I always have a small real

Christmas tree, but I haven't gotten it yet. Do you have your Christmas tree, Jill?''

"No," Jill said. "But I've been thinking about getting one. I wonder if you and I might go shopping for trees together.''

"When?" Elizabeth asked. "We probably should do it right away, since Christmas is only two weeks away—don't you think?''

Jill smiled up at Daniel. It would be their first Christmas together. "I think you're right, Elizabeth. Once the tree is up and decorated—''

"Then it's Christmas. Sanford loved Christmas— and he was so young when he died.'' Elizabeth continued talking but Jill's attention was on Daniel.

Something was wrong. Very wrong. Physically he was with them, smiling in sympathy as Elizabeth told them about the presents she'd never been able to give Sanford. But he was no longer with them.... He'd slipped into his private world, distanced himself from them.

He could be thinking about the prototype of a heating unit he was setting up in the farmhouse in Iowa, but instinctively she knew that was not true. Whatever he was thinking had to do with her, with them. But she was sure he would explain later, when they were alone.

"You're too young to think about your own mortality,'' Daniel said.

They were in Jill's apartment, sitting on the sofa closest to the window, looking at the valley lights. Both were tired after the outing to Tombstone. But not that tired, Jill thought.

She pivoted to face him. "Where did that come from?" she asked. "I asked if you had a problem you wanted to talk about."

"That's it," Daniel said. "Spending the day with the seniors made me think about my mortality. Where I fit into your life—"

"You are an integral part of it!"

"I'd have to know that what I could bring into a marriage would compensate for what living with me would mean you'd have to give up," he said.

"So tell me! What would I be giving up!"

"Children," he said. "I wouldn't want children. I wouldn't have the time to devote to them."

"I want to shake you until your brains rattle," Jill said. She laughed in spite of herself. He couldn't be serious. "Maybe you'd have a headache as big as the one you're giving me."

"You like honesty," he said wearily. "It's hurt your feelings now or later."

Jill collapsed into his arms. He tucked her close. He was trembling and she knew he was as devastated as she. He was going to sacrifice himself and her. Their happiness. But why?

"It doesn't make sense," she said. "A child of ours wouldn't lack love."

"It would lack time," he said. "I'm forty! By the time our first child graduated from high school, I'd be sixty. And look at Matthew."

"What does Matthew have to do with this?"

"He's sixty-two," Daniel said. "A male's average life span is, what—sixty-seven? I'd be lucky to live long enough to see my grandchildren born."

Jill sat, met his gaze. "You are making no sense at all," she said. "Your mother hasn't seen her grand-children born and you don't hear her—"

Suddenly he was gone, walking briskly to the door. "I'm sorry, Jill," he said. He looked back at her. "I need time to think this over."

"We'll talk tomorrow night," she stated.

"I'm flying to Iowa in the morning."

"You're running away from me," she said.

"Define it that way if you want," he said. "But I'm planning to do more work on the heating unit at the farm."

"You're running," Jill said firmly. "But it won't work out for you, Daniel. I'll be here when you need me."

She saw little of him over the next two weeks. After three days in Iowa, he had come back. But she had to learn from Belle that he had packed and flown to Chicago.

Maybe she had made herself too convenient, too available, too accessible. She had already started looking at trailers. Maybe she should step up the search. Put a little distance between them. Even a mile or two... Good grief. She was crazy. He had put distance between them.

Events at the center were moving at a breakneck pace as they headed into the Christmas holidays. Autry had asked Shauna to fly back to Iowa with Belle, Walter, Daniel and himself to meet the family. Daniel expected to be back from Chicago early on the twenty-third. They planned to leave at five o'clock on the same day.

She had to learn about it from Shauna.

Because Jill had taken a three-day Thanksgiving leave, she urged Shauna to go if she wanted. Shauna wanted. Phoebe and Ralph, knowing Jill would be alone on Christmas, had asked her to share Christmas dinner with them, as none of their own children was going to be able to come.

Down didn't describe what Jill was feeling. She danced a thin line between telling herself there had to be a reason for how Daniel was acting and an outright rage at the way he was shutting her out, not even giving her the opportunity to get to him.

What was happening now—though she tried to deny it—was that she was beginning to question the trust she had placed in Daniel.

She was in that frame of mind when Belle joined her on the evening of the twenty-second as she sat by the pool watching Chester take his nightly swim.

"There's a real chill in the air tonight," Belle observed. "I brought you a sweater."

Jill took the sweater and slipped it on. She had been chilled, but she'd been too deep in thought to realize it.

"Thank you," she said. "It feels good."

Belle pulled up a chair, settled on it. "I don't want to interfere," she said. "But I'm worried. You and Daniel seemed to have been feeling something very special for each other until the trip to Tombstone. Now all I see is unhappiness. Would you like to tell me why?"

Jill tried to smile. "What you see with me is called living in abject misery."

"You do love him," Belle said.

"Oh, yes, Belle. I do love him. And he loves me." It was such a relief to talk about it. Maybe she was too close to it. Maybe a third point of view would clarify matters. "But according to Daniel, loving me isn't enough. He talked about being forty, his mortality. He told me that he didn't want children."

"That doesn't sound like Daniel," Belle said thoughtfully. "He said nothing more?"

"He told me that he needed to think about us," Jill said. "Since then, he's managed to avoid me."

"It isn't like I hadn't noticed," Belle said. She patted Jill's hand. "Don't worry, dear. Daniel might be able to avoid you, but he has never been able to avoid me. Between the two of us, we'll snap him into shape."

Jill laughed. Maybe from relief. Maybe because she needed to laugh. She hadn't done much of that the past several weeks.

"Belle," she said, "I think you've been spending too much time with Nell and Phoebe."

"Oh, no," Belle laughed before adding thoughtfully, "Well, perhaps that is true. I'm *betting* Daniel spends Christmas with you."

Jill arrived back at the Holiday house after dark. Such a day, she thought. Shauna had left at noon to pack for the five-o'clock flight to Iowa.

She had no sooner gone when a man in his eighties began to complain about chest pains. He'd been taken by ambulance to the hospital. His wife had ridden with him. After closing the center, Jill had gone to the hospital to see whether or not there was something she could do.

She'd stayed until Nell arrived. Nell and Elizabeth were going to take turns staying with the woman until her children arrived. The children were in their sixties themselves. They had not been able to book a flight from where they lived in New Jersey, but had already left home, intending to drive straight through.

What a way to spend Christmas, Jill thought. But she was not going to think negatively. She was going to think of all the Christmases this family had shared.

How they would still share this one, even if it would be in a different way.

Back at the Holidays' she drove slowly up the driveway, hoping the Christmas lights Belle had hung on the cacti would be turned on, indicating that Daniel had had a change of heart and had decided to spend Christmas with her.

The whole place, outside of the yard light at the back of the house, was dark, but knowing Daniel wasn't here was not going to defeat her. She was going to think in a positive way. Sooner or later, Daniel had to face her.

In the meantime, she was going to enjoy the Christmas party at the center tomorrow. And dinner with Ralph and Phoebe on Christmas Day—if it killed her.

And it likely would. Daniel was more bullheaded than a mule. More unrelenting than a pit bull. More self-centered than Mrs. Chatham...and that was about as mean thinking as Jill could get.

In her heart she knew none of that was true.

What was true was that they belonged together. She was convinced it really had been her destiny to meet Daniel now. Just as destiny had kept them apart on the bike ride across Iowa so long ago.

But even then, they had been kindred spirits.

They were bonded. All he had to do was admit it, so they could move from this point, where Daniel was keeping all his hurt to himself, to the point where he would share it.

She parked in the garage. Before leaving the car, she took the flashlight from the glove compartment. The corner spotlights on Daniel's workshop didn't throw enough light into Chester's pen for her to see what she was doing.

Poor guy, she thought as she left to go and get him. As late as she was in coming to release him, he was bound to think he'd been deserted.

Like someone else she knew—someone who was not going to admit that was exactly how she felt. That a certain man in her life was slow to come around and in the meantime that person felt deserted.

Thinking about herself in the third person didn't cut it. Best to get her mind off Daniel or she would fall into a sulk and by the time he did get around to talking to her, she'd probably bop him for speaking to her.

She smiled at the thought. That was one way to get his attention. She flicked on the flashlight, opened the pen gate.

"Chester," she said. "I know I'm late. And I apologize for—" She spotted the hole where he'd burrowed under the fence. "Chester!"

She sent the light in a half circle, spotted a fast-moving, small black body at the back of the property. She ran in that direction, calling, "Chester! Get back here!" She whistled.

There was nothing to stop him. The security fence didn't cross the back of the property. Daniel had told her that was because the rough terrain protected it.

The flashlight beam danced erratically as she ran. First she would see Chester. Then she wouldn't. Then she saw his shadow as he darted into an outcrop of rock one hundred yards ahead of her.

She was panting, but he was not going to outrun her. Luckily she'd worn slacks and low heels today.

She lost track of him momentarily. "Chester? Chester?"

There was a quick movement to her left. He was running from the outcropping of rock, around a hedgehog cactus. She was in hot pursuit again. Why wasn't he coming to her? Was he sick? She avoided a jumping cholla. "Chester! Please! Stop!" But he didn't stop. He only ran farther into the foothills.

As Daniel pulled his car around the corner of the driveway, he saw what appeared to be a flashlight reflection at the back of the property. He parked, jumped from the car and rounded his workshop at the same time as Chester came from the pool.

In the distance he heard Jill calling. Chester responded to his name and started trotting into the darkness after her.

Daniel jogged in pursuit, going slowly, until his eyes adjusted to the darkness. What was Jill doing running toward the foothills calling for Chester when the pig was here?

Or at least somewhere ahead of him. "Jill! Wait up!" he called. "Chester's here." He called again. Blast the woman. If she would only shut up, she would hear him.

He ran a block in pursuit, cussed when his dress pants hooked the barbed spine of a prickly pear. He was going to be a walking pincushion before he caught up to her. He stopped, jerked the spine free and placed his hands to his mouth. "Jill! Stop where you are! Jill! Do you hear me?"

He saw the flash of a light perhaps a hundred yards ahead of him. "Daniel? Is that you?"

"Who in the hell else would be chasing a crazy woman around—"

"Can't talk! Chester's running away from me. He's not far ahead—"

"He's with me."

"No, he's—" Her voice rose an octave. "There are two of him! No! I mean two pigs!"

Daniel raced forward. She'd been chasing jabalina. "Don't go after them," Daniel called. "They're jabalina."

"Jabalina?"

"Small wild pigs. They can be vicious."

"I—oh! Daniel! Help me."

Daniel and Chester simultaneously reached Jill. She was sitting on the sand, directing the flashlight beam at her leg. He dropped down beside her.

"Did they attack you?" He shoved her hand away from where she was holding her ankle.

"Who?"

"The jabalina."

The flashlight shone in his face. "Why would you think that?"

"Possibly because you screamed, 'Help me, Daniel.'"

"Well, that's true enough—Chester," she said. She scratched him behind the ears, her voice all coddling and sweet. "Where were you?"

Daniel growled. "Good grief, Jill. Chester was taking his nightly dip. What was the 'Daniel, help me' thing?"

The light flashed in his eyes again. "Miss your flight?" When Daniel glowered, she said quickly, "I've got a jumping cholla spine sticking in my ankle."

"Of all the absolutely thoughtless things to do," Daniel snapped. "Don't you know how dangerous it is to be out alone in the foothills at night? That's really stupid."

"Yeah? Well, who is out here with me?" she snapped back. "Since you don't have to rescue me from jabalina, why don't you do something really chivalrous like taking the spine out of my leg?"

Daniel groped for her leg, started to roll her slacks
up. "It would help if you'd put the light on your leg.
That way I might be able to see what I'm doing."

She dropped the light to her leg. "If anyone here has
a right to be mad, Daniel Holiday, it's me. Not you!
And, ouch, that hurt!"

"You really did a job on yourself," he said. The
worry and concern had suddenly gone out of him.
"It's going to hurt. Hold still."

"Why are you here?"

He worked the spine free, tossed it aside, settled
back on his buttocks. He was grinning sheepishly
when she shone the light on him again. "Shut that
darn thing off, would you? The moon is bright enough
for us to see what we're doing."

She flicked off the flashlight. "I still haven't heard
why you're here," she said.

"At gate thirty-five before boarding for the nonstop flight back to Iowa—"

"I know the location," Jill said. "All I want are the
facts."

"My mother had a brief, pointed conversation with
me. She said she'd talked to you. You'd told her about
our last talk. My feeling about mortality and not
wanting children. She put two and two together and
came up with Dad."

"I thought all this had more to do with him than
us," Jill said. "So what did she say?"

"After I admitted that I had always feared dying
young because of Dad, Mother told me that kind of
thinking was—in her exact words—damn nonsense."

Jill gasped. "Your mother cussed?"

"Well, it looked like Mother and sounded like
Mother, so I have to conclude Mother cussed," he
said. He paused. "Dad had a congenital heart condition which at the time was deemed inoperable. They

had known about it for several years. They also had been assured that his condition was not inheritable. I always thought it had to be something like that," he concluded. "That's why I stopped in Rochester on my way to Chicago to have a thorough physical."

"And you're fit as a fiddle," Jill said.

"Are you a doctor, too?" Daniel teased.

"No," she said suggestively. "But I do know about your physical prowess."

"Jill," Daniel said. "You make it awfully darn hard to concentrate. Now do you want to hear what Mother said, or not?"

"You did it for me, didn't you, Daniel?" Jill asked. "Stopped in Rochester for that physical."

"I did it because of you," he said.

Jill slid to his side, placed her hand over his where it lay on the sand. He had more to say. "Continue," she offered.

"I'm a man filled with fear. I've made an art of procrastinating," Daniel said softly. "But you knew that."

"I knew."

"Fear kept me from asking Mother about my dad. Fear kept me from allowing her to bring the subject up for an airing. Fear kept me from admitting that I loved you. I don't know how easy fear is to shake."

"You don't have to shake it, Daniel. Just share it. Did your mother have anything else to say about your father?"

"She knew my father loved me," Daniel said. "But he didn't know how to express it. And when he learned how ill he was, he worried about his kids a lot. She asked me to think about what he was *really* saying when he would warn me that my daydreaming could lead to hurting someone."

"And?"

"Mother asked why I was flying to Iowa when I wanted to be with you."

"And?" Jill said.

"I had to confess that I was still fearful, still running, but the time had come to admit it. I thought about my relationship with Dad all the way from Sky Harbor. I think Dad did love me. I think he was trying to warn me that he wouldn't always be around to protect me."

Jill sighed. She was forgiving Daniel's father. "I like that interpretation."

"So," he said abruptly. "I am still forty."

"Such a pessimist I'm going to marry—"

"Did I ask?" Daniel laughed.

"I'm sure I heard you," Jill said. "Back somewhere when you were talking about your physical." She rested her head on his shoulder. "I can see us now, Daniel. We're eighty. Sitting on the front porch watching your grandchildren play. We're whispering back and forth. You wonder which will take after you and tinker. I wonder which will take after me and be a do-gooder."

"I was wrong about that call," Daniel said huskily. "You're a caretaker of hearts. And right now, this moment my heart still concerns me. I'm very much in need of a hug."

The hug developed into a kiss. The kiss deepened.

"I have a theory," Jill murmured. "A wonderful, workable theory. It begins, actions speak—"

"And ends—louder than words," he said, easing her back to the sand.

*   *   *   *   *

COMING NEXT MONTH

#832   ARC OF THE ARROW—Rita Rainville
Written in the Stars
Brandy Cochran thought accountants were quiet and dull—but no one could accuse R. G. Travers of being boring! The sexy Sagittarian's determined pursuit made her nervous . . . but so did the idea of life without him. . . .

#833   THE COWBOY AND THE CHAUFFEUR—Elizabeth August
Rachel Hadley hadn't expected much from life, but rugged cowboy Logan James was determined to change that. He swept the cool chauffeur out of the driver's seat and into the arms of love—his arms!

#834   SYDNEY'S FOLLY—Kasey Michaels
Sydney Blackmun's latest ''project'' was getting the oh-so-serious Blake Mansfield involved in Ocean City's surfside fun. But could she convince her new neighbor that their love was more than a summer folly?

#835   MISTLETOE AND MIRACLES—Linda Varner
Being trapped with playboy author Matt Foxx was *not* efficiency expert Kirby Gibson's idea of a merry Christmas. Matt broke every rule she had, but how could Kirby resist a man who kissed so well?

#836   DONE TO PERFECTION—Stella Bagwell
Caterer Julia Warren knew how she'd like to serve all lawyers—well-done! But Judge Harris Hargrove was determined to prove that he was to Julia's taste. . . .

#837   TOO GOOD TO BE TRUE—Victoria Glenn
Ashli Wilkerson didn't know why she was upset that real-estate developer Kyle Hamilton was engaged to her sister—she didn't even *like* the man! But liking had little to do with loving. . . .

AVAILABLE THIS MONTH:

FOUR UNIQUE SERIES
FOR EVERY WOMAN YOU ARE...

Silhouette Romance®

Tender, delightful, provocative—stories that capture the laughter, the tears, the *joy* of falling in love. Pure romance...straight from the heart!

SILHOUETTE *Desire*®

Go wild with Desire! Passionate, emotional, sensuous stories of fiery romance. With heroines you'll like and heroes you'll *love,* Silhouette Desire never fails to deliver.

Silhouette Special Edition®

Stories of love and life, these powerful novels are tales that you can identify with—romances with "something special" added in! Silhouette Special Edition is entertainment for the heart.

SILHOUETTE·INTIMATE·MOMENTS™

Enter a world where passions run hot and excitement is the rule. Dramatic, larger-than-life and always compelling—Silhouette Intimate Moments will never let you down.

This is the season of giving, and Silhouette proudly offers you its sixth annual Christmas collection.

SILHOUETTE

Christmas Stories

1991

Experience the joys of a holiday romance and treasure these heart-warming stories by four award-winning Silhouette authors:

Phyllis Halldorson—"A Memorable Noel"
Peggy Webb—"I Heard the Rabbits Singing"
Naomi Horton—"Dreaming of Angels"
Heather Graham Pozzessere—"The Christmas Bride"

Discover this yuletide celebration—sit back and enjoy Silhouette's Christmas gift of love.